Phoenix

IRISH SHORT STORIES 2001

Phoenix **IRISH**
SHORT STORIES
2001

edited by David Marcus

PHŒNIX

First published in Great Britain in 2001 by Phoenix, a division of

The Orion Publishing Group Ltd
Orion House
5 Upper Saint Martin's Lane
London WC2H 9EA

A CIP catalogue record for this book is available
from the British Library

ISBN 0 75381304 1

Typeset at The Spartan Press Ltd,
Lymington, Hants
Printed by The Guernsey Press Co Ltd,
Guernsey, C.I.

ACKNOWLEDGEMENTS

None of the following stories has previously appeared in print.

'Miami Vice', Copyright © Kevin Barry, 2001; 'Weir Way', Copyright © Michael Carragher, 2001; 'The Destruction Test', Copyright © John Fleming, 2001; 'Halcyon Day', Copyright © Jane S. Flynn, 2001; 'Vodka on Sunday', Copyright © Fiona Gartland, 2001; 'The Máistir', Copyright © William Hodder, 2001; 'Linguini', Copyright © Cormac James, 2001; 'The Purple Dahlia', Copyright © Mary Leland, 2001; 'Time', Copyright © Seán MacMathúna, 2001; 'Hatteras', Copyright © Molly McCloskey, 2001; 'Pane Barrier', Copyright © Brian McKillop, 2001; 'Roles', Copyright © Gillman Noonan, 2001; 'The Grandfathers', Copyright © Augustus Young, 2001; 'The Bestiary', Copyright © William Wall, 2001.

'Pale Hands I Loved Beside the Shalimar', Copyright © Anne Enright, 2001, previously appeared in *The Paris Review*; 'An Evening Out', Copyright © William Trevor, 2001, previously appeared in *Tatler* (UK).

CONTENTS

Introduction by David Marcus   ix

SEÁN MacMATHÚNA Time   1
BRIAN McKILLOP Pane Barrier   13
MOLLY McCLOSKEY Hatteras   23
GILLMAN NOONAN Roles   32
WILLIAM TREVOR An Evening Out   40
KEVIN BARRY Miami Vice   59
JOHN FLEMING The Destruction Test   69
WILLIAM HODDER The Máistir   76
CORMAC JAMES Linguini   89
WILLIAM WALL The Bestiary   99
AUGUSTUS YOUNG The Grandfathers   139
MARY LELAND The Purple Dahlia   144
FIONA GARTLAND Vodka on Sunday   161
MICHAEL CARRAGHER Weir Way   167
ANNE ENRIGHT Pale Hands I Loved Beside the Shalimar   187
JANE S. FLYNN Halcyon Day   198

Biographical Notes   207

INTRODUCTION

When compiling the biographical notes of the contributors to this issue, I was struck by the fact that seven of the sixteen were born in Cork City or County. Cork City being my own birthplace, it was only natural that I would experience a frisson of pride at this discovery, but what gave me as much pleasure was the evidence that the heritage of three of Ireland's greatest short-story writers of the past, also Cork-born – Daniel Corkery (his four collections regrettably long out of print), Sean O'Faolain and Frank O'Connor – was still alive.

Reflecting particularly on the stories of O'Connor and O'Faolain, I recalled their contrasting attitudes to the craft employed in the short story, especially to the importance of revision. The former would revise a story again and again before publication – no doubt the latter would too – but O'Connor continued revising a story even after it was published, sometimes for years afterwards. O'Faolain regarded this practice as a species of literary forgery.

Be that as it may, too many aspiring writers of short stories appear to think that revision consists of cosmetic alterations made during the process of composition. The younger the writer, the more likely this belief, possibly because a young, articulate writer, finding his or her words flowing so easily, mistakes spontaneity for inspiration. But beware – both spontaneity and inspiration can be very dangerous infections for a writer without knowledge of or recourse to their antidote: the morning-after pill of revision.

For Frank O'Connor a real writer should revise a story endlessly, though perhaps hardly to the extent of producing thirty-six new versions, the number he is said to have written over the years of one of his already-published stories. For the young writer, O'Connor's 'endlessly' should amount to more than one revision over a reasonable length of time *after* the story has ostensibly been finished. That is the only way the writer can engineer and exploit the necessary opportunities to bring a story to life. Creation is only the birth, maturation the full growth; and for a story to achieve maturation, every one of its elements, from initial seed to final length, must be rigorously interrogated if the story is to be as perfectly formed as possible.

I would add that when the writer has fulfilled all his or her obligations to the short story, one further, but never mentioned obligation remains: the reader's. The short story is regarded as fiction's poetry, but what poetry lover reads a poem only once? The once-round-the-block reader of a short story is selling himself, and the story, short.

David Marcus

Time

It was just what a prison should be, a building in a wilderness. All round it layers of heather, above it layers of larks, whose layers of song drew faces up from the exercise yard. That was outside. Inside was the wilderness of solitary footfalls, of clanging steel, of guttural echoes.

There was a knock at the door behind him and in came the assistant chief. 'Letter for you, Mr Crean, addressed to The Prison, Achamurry, just like before. We like to call it a Facility for Offenders, not prison – no offence!'

Crean nodded, took the letter and tore it open. He had been through this before and he explained it again: she was doing it to humiliate him, wouldn't write to his home address. The assistant thought about it but decided he didn't want to get involved in a family argument.

'They'll be here shortly in dribs and drabs. Broken schedules today, I fear.' And he was gone.

Crean read the letter quickly, to get it over with more than anything else. As he suspected, there was no mention of his son in it, although he had begged for news of him in his last letter. She hadn't got a phone yet! Oh, she was a cute one! It was already a month and he was gasping for his seven-year-old, the tinkle of his voice would do beautifully.

'What's it going to be today, Dan?' said a voice behind him.

He turned round and there was Culligan standing by the door with a few books under his arm.

'Maybe we'll read a bit of a poem,' said Crean. Culligan was in for a double murder, his wife and her father, one day after a pub row. Why? Because they had been laughing at him. 'They won't laugh no more,' was all he would say, 'and that's for fuckin' sure.' He didn't have a nail left on his finger: neither did he have a friend, for he had threatened almost everybody that he would do them when he got out.

'A poem!' he said. He was outraged as he searched Crean's eyes for deliberate intent to persecute. 'I don't go for no poems, don't give a rattling frig for poems, none o' that shit, like, know what I mean?'

'We'll make it a short one,' said Crean and he didn't give a rattling frig either. Culligan stared at Crean for ages before he decided he wasn't being insulted and sat down.

Crean dumped a few books out of his bag. One was the works of Paddy Kavanagh. Kavanagh had eleven poems that were as good as any other eleven in the world – he was sure of that. After that you were groping in the stew for bits of stringy mutton. Same with all poets. Eleven.

There it was again, the letter; after she had had the house, the furniture, the goddamned dog even, three pages of accounts and whining about money. Damn it to hell! Where was Adrian, didn't she know what a crap heap he was working in! There was nothing in his life, all he wanted was the kid, only a loan, god-damn it, say for an afternoon. But first he'd kiss the head off him, then hug him and feel all the coldness of the last three months drain away, drain away. The goddamn bitch! And he kicked the radiator, causing a metal clunk to travel all the way down the prison.

'Oh, now sir, sir, sir, what are we doing, kicking the prison furniture? Department of Justice no like!' Cooney, the embezzler, came in and sat beside Culligan, then changed his mind and went back a seat.

'You're always fuckin' doin' that, Cooney,' said Culligan. 'It's fuckin' insultin', isn't it, Dan?'

'Yeah, insultin',' said Crean, who felt like throwing himself out the window. Only they were already on the ground, in a Nissen hut. The prison people could never make up their minds as to whether they wanted a schoolhouse or not. And he didn't give a 'rattling frig' about that either.

'Culligan,' said Cooney, 'you shot a pair, I don't want to sit with nobody that shot a pair, bad luck!' Cooney, who called himself an accountant, had never really qualified but was a natural who went from minding the till to book-keeping and then to financial deals and self-aggrandisement, embezzling close to a million which was never recovered; but they said he kept a map of Switzerland in his cell. They gave him six years for not telling and for having his wife and kids living in luxury. This he proved to everybody by showing the photographs: everybody had a peek. His wife Nannia – yeah, Nannia – looked sexy with the kids in the new extension in Foxrock. He used to boast about the sentence. 'Not fair, six years, six years in Ireland is longer than twelve years in Australia, time dilation they call it, it's the weather, it's true, honest, in the Irish language time and weather are the same word, that right, Dan?'

Crean didn't answer because at that moment he had decided he hated the place and everyone in it. And yet he liked them. That was a contradiction, and that's the way it was in this place, day and night the contradictions crashing in his mind.

'Frawley's not comin' any more, you only gave him four outa ten for his essay,' said Kinnear, whose large bulk filled the doorway. In each sweaty hand there was a box of tissues.

'You tell Frawley to go and fuck himself,' said Crean, throwing books around his desk, 'and in case you think that was a misprint, tell him to go fuck himself.'

'Great news,' said Culligan. 'That Frawley gives me the fuckin' creeps.'

Cooney nodded in agreement. 'Gettin' crowded here anyway,' he said.

Crean bit his lip: this was the first time he'd used the f word in class openly. He sighed; foul-mouthedness round here was built into the walls. Tim Dawley, the chaplain, had resisted it for years, but now he effed and blinded non-stop and the bishop had told him he couldn't send him anywhere else so he was there for keeps. This was it, a prison was a grasping evil that wasn't satisfied with just the condemned; anyone who touched its walls, even the visitors, felt its encircling tentacles.

Kinnear advanced into the room, examining all the seats, even sniffing them, before he chose one almost under Crean's desk. He was in for rape, and he would only rape seventeen-year-old schoolgirls in uniform. He was out every five years and went straight for a uniform, and back he came. It was no use shouting at him, 'Why school uniforms, can't you go for a nurse or something?' He would throw up his hands and say, 'How do I know, we don't know who we are, nobody alive knows who he is, I feel I'm somebody else, so, he's the guy to ask.' He wasn't disliked for this, for prisoners found it easy to forgive a man his predominant passions; in prison it was the little things that got to them, like Kennear's obsession with health and cleanliness.

Crean looked at the letter again. Each time he looked at it he discovered a new level. Suddenly he became scared. This was not her style, this was pure legalese and it was typed. Who'd type it for her? Christ, the boyfriend might be a lawyer, that was it. Crean looked at his watch. It was too early to go sick, he'd have to wait until after lunch.

Frawley strolled into the room with O'Sullivan, the fisherman. The fisherman went to the back and rolled a fag. Frawley sat on the edge of Crean's desk. 'You only gave me four outa ten, Dan,

Jesus Christ, I'm worth five at least.' Crean buried his face in his hands.

'Give the fucker five or we'll be here all day,' shouted Cooney.

Crean walked to the window and peered through the gateway at the morning haze. Moor browns, heath browns, bog browns, fox browns, all stretching away into the distance. Overhead the clouds looked as if they had been put there by the prison architects. 'Weary, man,' was all he whispered. He took the essay from Frawley and threw down a mark of ten out of ten and handed it back to him.

'Ten outa ten, Jack, for taking it all down from the encyclopedia, no mistakes.' Frawley sat down happily and waved his essay in the air.

'I have to be careful of my image, Dan, I'm not a robber, I'm a real classy fence, a man of taste and culture.' And so he was. He was very fond of old Irish Georgian silver, which he found very difficult to part with. Pity he hadn't stuck to it, for he had been caught with a painting. 'This dirty big painting, bigger'n the blackboard there, by some fucker called Keating, crossing the street with it, didn't have a chance.'

'Can we get on with the Leaving Cert course, I want to get on,' said Kinnear.

'You want to get on another schoolgirl, you mean, you bollix,' screamed Culligan. But Kinnear insisted, 'I want to get my Leaving Cert. What's up today, Dan?'

'We'll read Kavanagh's poem *Memory of my Father*.'

'Is it on the course, will it come up?' asked Cooney.

'I don't want to do no poem,' shouted Culligan. 'It reminds me of school.'

'You're in school, here!' said Frawley.

'No, I'm not, this is no school, Dan there doesn't know one end of a blackboard from the other, that right, Dan?'

Crean squinted through the window again; it was the same

landscape except that any moment there would be a cloudburst. You could rely on this landscape and its cardinal points – rain from the west, cold sunshine from the south, letters and visitors from the east, and at night moonlight and cats competing for the window sills. He pretended to read his letter but really worried about his relationship with the prisoners. If you got too palsy-walsy with them they'd piss all over you. It called for command.

'Get this clear, I'm running this show, you will do as I say, leave the exam to me and you'll get it. If you don't like that go now, otherwise shut up. Page fifty-nine,' he said quietly. There was a hurried rustle of pages.

To prisoners poems were official documents that needed to be scanned to find the bad news. That took a lot of rustling paper and moving lips. That's when the thunderclap shook the whole prison and everyone jumped. Thunder in a prison is scarier than anywhere else, for prisoners feel that God doesn't love them. Then lightning making the shadows flay each other, followed by an awesome silence. Another thunderclap brought pursed lips and rain bucketing down on the felt roof. The door flew open below and in came an elderly traveller, dripping water.

'Please, teacher, can I take a bita shelter, I'm soakin',' he asked. All the students turned and glared at him. Growls escaped from them. 'Go find someplace else,' and 'Piss off!'

'You're OK, sit on the chair there near the door,' Crean shouted down to him. He had seen the man earlier in the yard picking up oak leaves that late autumn blew over the prison walls. He eyed the class, but not reproachfully, he knew the reflex, having seen it often in the past. They just did not like types – rich types, poor types, tall types, small types, bog types, mountain types, travel-ling types, immobile types, anybody who wasn't their type. And what type was that? The meek, who were waiting to inherit the earth.

'Right, then, here goes,' said Crean. 'I'll read it nice and easy.'

When he finished, Crean was pleased with the way he had read it, no histrionics, just natural with the rhythm and wisdom of a man who knew that feelings were more important than ideas. He looked at the class – they were totally unmoved. He told them about the poet and his novel *Tarry Flynn*, about his magazine, about *The Green Fool*, about drinking in Baggot Street, lots of things. He spoke about the faces of old men that haunt us all with their compassion for a cruel world. He spoke of the wisdom of fathers – but to no avail, they just looked at the ground, in a mannerly sort of way. He read it again, this time with panache – he loved that word. But they were unmoved.

He glanced down at the letter. That's when his mind did a curious flip. If Adrian, his son, were to read this poem in twenty years' time, what would he have to say about his father? Panic suddenly took hold of Crean as clashing views and images of his son raced into his mind. He'd say his father had walked away from him, uncaring, selfish, a deadbeat dad! His mother would have taken care of the image process, censoring his letters, maybe burning them, and carefully building up in the child's mind an unfavourable view of Crean. It would be so easy; she had the time, the intelligence, the intent.

The panic got worse as he felt the isolation of his position. These panics had appeared from nowhere about a month after the separation. They were getting worse. Desperately his mind sought a defence. Was there anything coming up, something nice, today, tonight? Which made him think of Murty's! The local pub! A pissing hell, full of rattleheads who took turns at being the village idiot. Murty's! From now on it would be all downhill and don't spare the horses.

There was an interruption from the bottom of the class.

'Teacher, that was a nice verse, it made me think,' said the traveller. Crean and the rest of the class gazed down at the weather-beaten face of this fifty-plus-year-old soaking beside the door. It might provide the escape he needed.

'Think what?' he asked.

'I was thinkin' that poetry is grand but smell is stronger.'

'Smell!'

'Yeah, the other day I had to clean out the wood shed. There was a tar barrel there. I took off the lid and smelt the inside. It was like a mule kicking me in the chest, for it brought me back to my childhood and my father. We were badly off in those days, we lived in a wood in tar barrels. The smell of that barrel made me travel a fair distance, sir.'

The class looked at each other and then started to roar out laughing. 'Tar barrels!' Crean couldn't stop himself either.

Frawley sneered. 'Your own tar barrel! Did you have one all to yourself?'

'No, I was with the dog.'

Cooney jumped up. 'Don't laugh, detached residence, not overlooked, in a sylvan setting, needing some refurbishing!' This set everybody off again. The traveller took it all in good part and smiled at everyone happily. Woe to the honest, said Crean to himself, for that's what they were laughing at, his honesty.

'It's true,' said Crean, 'it's little things like tar that have the power of memory. What reminds you guys of your fathers?' He walked through their seats as they thought about it. 'A photo, a book, a walking stick? Every time I see an Airedale terrier I think of my dad, he used to breed them. Take your time, figure it out, get in touch, and we'll talk about it.'

Already he felt better. He was drawn to the window again, and he knew why – he could see out through the gate to the country beyond. Because for the first time since he came here the place was getting to him. It was not so much the encroachment of space, more the oppression of time – for in here time seemed not to move.

The lightning became more frequent, making all the faces deadly pale and causing little bursts of shadow to run round the room. Rolls of thunder seemed to bring a strange silence. He looked down at the envelope again. John Crean, The Prison! Prison! With his biro he drew bars across the envelope. He was in prison, she had him incarcerated! He could almost see her smile as she wrote it.

He sat at the table in front of them and looked at the concentrating faces. 'Well, how're we doin', guys, any little stories?' There was no reply, which was unusual for such a garrulous bunch. He turned to Kinnear. 'How about you, Tim?' Kinnear made as if to speak, then changed his mind and just shrugged.

'Maybe you'd rather not?'

Kinnear, who always wanted to be helpful, didn't like that. 'A letter,' he said.

'From your dad?'

'The week before he died.' There was a heaviness about the words.

'It's a very important letter, then.'

It took ages for him to reply and when he did there was a catch in his voice. 'In the letter he said he,' – here he looked around at Frawley and the others – 'He said he forgave me!'

'Is that important?' Crean asked. What a stupid question! Something had changed. He looked around and slowly realised that he had pushed them too far. Fathers run deep in us all, deep, deep, the ancient deep, and therefore powerful. And dangerous.

'Okay, we can move on fr . . .' he said, but he was interrupted by a chair falling over. Culligan was up and gathering his books.

'What the fuck's going on here, huh? What's all this crap about my father? Do you know where you are, this is a fuckin' prison, not a psychiatric ward.' He put his books under his arm. 'I'm outa here! You think I give a shit about him?' He glared fiercely at everybody. 'Know what he did to me? As a child. Wanna know? No, you fuckin' don't! So, what's all this crap about? If it weren't for him I'd . . .' He suddenly seemed defeated and his gaze fell. 'What's the use?' is all he said, and he walked out of the classroom.

There was only one question on Crean's mind: why today, why did everything have to fall on his head today? He looked at the book and the papers on his desk and tried to figure out where he'd go from here.

O'Sullivan, the fisherman, got up and gathered his books. 'Dan, I can't think of home, it's too far away. I don't mean distance, I mean time. Years, Christ, and for what, I did nothing. I can't take it, Dan.'

Everybody liked O'Sullivan, for his trusting qualities and friendliness. But with qualities like that he needed protection in a prison. His family had hired a vicious type from the Liberties to keep an eye on him. He was in for a drug haul in his boat, but all the prisoners knew he had been done. He was trusting. 'If he was a woman he'd be raped. Often,' Kinnear had volunteered. Cooney could take his boat off him. He had two worries, one that all the fish would be cleared by Spanish trawlers by the time he got out, the second was missing his father, who was getting old and might find managing the boat heavy going. A distant flash lit up his troubled face.

'I'm going to woodwork class, it's all this, this, you know, poems, all about, about, home, home, can't take it, no hard feelings, Dan.'

He didn't bang the door like Culligan, but he went all the same. O'Sullivan was right, woodwork wouldn't mess around with the soul, all you needed was a pair of hands and a hammer.

'Who's next for woodwork?' Crean asked with a smile. After a while Cooney muttered that his father had never visited him; and that it was important to know where you stood. He said he'd be back the next day. Kinnear nodded weakly to Dan and shuffled out. Frawley said he loved his father and would do another essay on Georgian silver, and this time he'd be looking for a six at least. And that was that, nobody left but the traveller.

Crean walked all around the room waiting for a decision about his life to fall out of the sky, one that would get him the hell out of there. He stopped in front of the traveller. 'You miss the barrel?' he asked. The man shook his head and smiled.

'But nice memories?'

'A few that would be hard to get rid of. He used to beat me. But only when he got drunk.' Crean found himself examining the man, especially the hands and face. Every inch of them bore scars of one kind or another.

'You've been beaten a lot since then!'

'Beaten, yes, but never bet.' Beaten, never bet! Kavanagh would have loved the phrase. And then he had to admit that the traveller and the poet had a lot in common: an innocence, an innocence that was so powerful that Crean could only feel an outraged humility in the presence of this huge soul. He sat down beside him.

'I'm having a bad day. It's my son,' said Crean. The other man looked at him strangely.

'What is it?'

'Broke up, my wife has him, and I'm here.'

'But he's alive.'

'Of course he's alive!'

'So you'll see him again!'

'Of course I'll see him.'

'And you'll have him all your life.'

'I suppose so.'

'Then everything's fine.'

Now it was Crean's turn to look strangely at him. 'Were

you . . . did you have . . . ?' My God, he said to himself, he's been hit from both sides, father and son.

The traveller got up and stamped the floor a few times. He paused at the door. 'It's nice to have something to miss,' was all he said, and then left.

Crean looked round the room to make sure he was on his own. He was. He knew he had just had a brush with the underbelly of humanity, and in a strange way he felt better about the world, Adrian, the prison, his awful wife, literature, the lot. He felt liberated from, from what, from the oppressive view that all things must work comfortably at all times.

The roof was leaking again. He looked up at it. A few days ago he had been doing haikus with the class, Japanese three-line poems. One had been

> *drip, drip, drip*
> *the prison roof –*
> *eternity leaking*

Good, let it!

BRIAN McKILLOP

Pane Barrier

Settled in his chair at last, the heat of a mug in the hollow of his hands, Steen closed his eyes and with a sigh let the mingled tones of the darkness and the warmth permeate him. From his clothes, the cold scent of the autumnal air still fresh and crisp appeased him. The sounds of the street beyond, the manic toots and salutes of horns, the tout and trade of voices, were growing fainter, ever fainter, in his mind. He stretched forth his legs and softened his back in the folds. A sudden crack against the windowpane startled him unduly. An orphaned twig twisting in the wind. Turning his chair towards the window he lit a cigarette, lay back and, letting his eyes glide softly, wandered in his mind.

Above and beyond dark clouds, large bloated faces as to the season astir with a tear, loomed menacingly. Before him in countless rows the backs of houses. Grey by grey into the horizon. Beneath, small ivy-strewn walls separated tiny gardens, wretched little islands weary and smothering under domestic castaways. Agrow here and there an ill-branched tree. On a wall here and there a cat in the curl. Evening had fallen. Soon it would be night. Soon what little light there was would fade into shadow and the window would once again reflect back upon himself the bewraying image of his own face.

He was about to slide the chair back to the centre of the room and make a start on a letter when by chance his eye happened to catch what appeared to be a figure by a window some distance away. The figure, it now seemed to him, of a woman. Watching him. Or was she? Perhaps he was being vain. Perhaps she was reading a book. Either way he couldn't be sure, but the longer he looked the more he felt certain it was a woman. Though the features were indistinguishable something about the shape of the head, something about the set of the shoulders, convinced him that it had to be. Those hints of blue, surely the straps to a gown. And yes! He could see the hair now. Dark about the shoulders. Straight, it seemed. Or was it shadows? No, no, it was hair. Dark, long, luxuriant hair. Fastened by a bobble more than likely. True, there were of course men with such hair, men with such shoulders, men who wore bobbles, but none with such a posture. Men did not sit in such a way. Men did not sit like her.

A dead ash fell upon his knee. He blew it to the floor without breaking gaze. How could he? She was enchanting. A figure of beauty framed within the dull. And how like a portrait he had once perceived, the when and the whereabouts of which he could not now recall. So delicate the tilt of the head on the lean neck. The look vague, a little wistful. Not a movement. Wrapped in the warm dreams of quiescence. How had his eyes failed to notice her before?

He made to take a last puff from the cigarette but it was dead, burnt out between his fingers. How long had he been staring? What did it matter. Could the eyes betray? Fastened, they were, and would remain just as long as he wished – as she wished. For perhaps it was her wish. Perhaps she could see him just as he could see her. Not clearly, but of course not. That would lack mystery. Intrigue. How cunning women were! A dark cloud passed and stole her from him, not entirely but enough to encase her in shadow. No more was visible to him now than a mere outline. Soon it would be night. For a time he retained his gaze, hopeful, expectant, anticipating a light from within her room that might serve to enshrine her as before. But nothing came. Nothing. Only darkness.

For some time he sat in darkness, rocking on the hind legs of the chair, the image that had taken form before his eyes still alive in his mind; now dressed, now undressed, by a tree, by the sea, in an alley, in a valley, hand in hand in dilly-dally. She was his now. She belonged to him. A faceless lady upon whom he could paint whatever face he wished. How they flashed through his mind! Followed by features, looks, postures, glances, smiles, smiles aplenty, aye, and moans, deep, long, frenzied moans, akin to those of amour. His eyes fell away from the window. Night had fallen.

He leant across to the little table in the centre of the room and turned on the lamp. The warm beam dazzled his eyes. Was it possible she could have taken that for a signal? Lighthouse, Morse Code, that kind of thing. Maybe. He turned the lamp off again. Waited. Nothing. He turned it on, off once more, then finally on again. Silly. She was gone. He lay back in the chair and stretched. The letter could wait until tomorrow. Tomorrow! Would she be by the window again?

He hooked a foot behind the leg of the little table and dragged it across to the ledge. Feet thus propped he lit another cigarette and took to blowing smoke-rings in the air. Suddenly he became conscious of his position. With the light now on it was as though he were naked in a spotlight. Should she still be espying him from the shadows how must he look to her now? A slouch. Slowly he slid his back to an upright position in the chair, but at once felt very rigid. Like a predator concealed in shadows it was as though those eyes from afar were boring through him. That profile of himself which he had never liked now lay before her. That nose. He wanted to turn and face the window but somehow could not. To move now would appear too obvious, obvious of the need to move. He would look simply foolish to just up and rise. Fool! What was he thinking? What was he saying to himself? In all probability she was gone, and if not what matter? It was quite possible she had not even so much as noticed him. She was hardly a spy. Indeed, if anyone could be accused of spying it was he. It was he whose wild eyes had stared so intently. So indiscreetly! What if she had misconstrued? A pervert! A madman! What if even now she was hurrying to alert the attention of some other? More, what if she were summoning the very police themselves? An anxious hand made for the blinds and pulled them fast. A madman!

He sat for a moment at war with a ragnail. Was it . . . yes . . . it was possible. He stubbed out the cigarette and stood up, with the idea of leaving the room, the house; then sat down immediately. No. He was being ridiculous. Utterly ridiculous. The abrupt slam of a door from somewhere down below startled him. He heard the sound of voices rising upwards from the hallway beneath. Whose? They seemed heated. Loud. Almost aggressive. With a sudden leap he sprang from the chair and hurried to the door. His instinct was to lock it instantly but instead, ever so gently, he opened it and listened through the crack. Someone laughed. Another door opened then quickly closed and the voices faded. From the adjacent room a man now appeared. He paused in the doorway before shutting it behind him. A pair of thick dark eyebrows frowned before passing. Steen waited until the man's footsteps were no longer audible on the stairs, then gently pulled the door to a close. Once more inside his room, he let his body fall limply on to the bed and, throwing back his head, laughed a little sigh or sighed a little laugh. His stomach rumbled under a yawn. Of the two choices, food or sleep, sleep seemed best. If she was by the window again tomorrow it might mean she was interested. Maybe not. He stripped off his clothes and slipped in under the sheets. As he switched off the lamp an afterglow of light remained before his eyes. He closed his eyes but the light remained within his mind and formed, through colours unseen by open eyes, an image. Her image. His image.

*

It was late in the morning before he awoke, weary and addled from a protracted sleep. Now and then through the slits in the blinds a ray of sunlight entered and left. At last one lingered and he raised the sheets. He made his way to the bathroom, dressed and, returning, set the kettle on the boil. Moving to the window, he drew open the blinds and gazed out against the light. His eyes wandered over the many houses, the many windows, seeking the one, which now located seemed much nearer than it had appeared the night before. The curtains were still undrawn. There sat the chair by the window, but nobody occupied it now. Instead, in its place, a bunch of clothes in various colours and styles lay strewn in a heap. He flipped the latch from the rung and edged it forth a nip. Beyond, in the window opposite, a man now emerged into frame, his face turned from view, and began to take down a picture from the wall. He disappeared suddenly only to reappear again, this time frontwise before the window. A small cap rested on his crown. He raised his face to the fore and fastened his glare directly. Steen mirrored his gaze for some seconds before relinquishing his attention to the kettle. Who on earth was this man?

That there could be another, amorous or other, in the life of the lady of the shadows Steen had never considered. Now, as he stirred to a colour his coffee, faint eddies of excitement made him somewhat anxious. The man by the window appeared old, too old to be anyone other than a father, say, or an uncle or perhaps a fellow lodger or, better still, the landlord. If he was the landlord that would certainly explain his presence in the room, but of course that did not discount the possibility of the other three or indeed the fourth, a husband or boyfriend.

The rumble of an engine from somewhere down below stalled his thoughts. He lifted his coffee and moved back before the pane. A rickety old van had pulled into the yard and come to a halt close beneath the window opposite. Steen looked from the van to the window, the window to the van, and back again. There stood the man with the cap as before. He had now gathered together the clothes from the chair and assembled them in a bundle in his arms. With these he vanished again from view. A new thought now entered Steen's mind, namely this: that if these two characters, the man with the cap in the room above and the man below, who had just stepped out of the van, were one and the same, in the sense of being two colleagues – a pair of painters perhaps – then it was possible that the lady in question was having her rooms made over during her absence. Or perhaps she, like him, had just moved to the city and was having her belongings transferred from her previous address to her new one or, worse, the opposite was true and she was moving not in but out and those pensive eyes of the night preceding were the very results of such. That the man below who emerged from the van was attired in the odds and ends of a tradesman seemed to confirm the fact that these two men had been called upon to do a job, that and nothing more.

Steen looked back to the window, but there was no sign of the man with the cap. The man below, however, an old fellow with a hucklebacked walk, was now busy shuffling to and opening the doors at the rear of the van. After this laborious exertion he settled his rump on the back of the van and planted a pipe in his mouth. With a deep prolonged puff his features crumpled into a most unhealthy and harmonious union with the rest of his appearance, which was that of a poor bastard tied to the crupper of a horse and trundled through the wilds of the country. Gratitude and great satisfaction coloured his cheeks. The man with the cap now emerged from a door carrying the clothes in the crib of his arms. Among these sweet and sundries, all in the feminine fold, were items of lingerie: knickers, garters and bras, whose combination as a whole had fashioned a great sweeping smile on the face of El Carrier, which now instantly transferred itself with all the invisible intensity of a virus to the old man with the pipe, so setting his head rocking and bobbing like a buoy on a wave. This rocking and bobbing increased itself no end when the old man looked to the foot of the man with the cap and perceived that a bra had fastened itself like a leech to his shin. Sensing something amiss, Sweets of the Bounty looked to his hoof, paused a second for the sake of effect, then drew back his boot and with a grave swing shot the bra up through the air, where, catching in the wind, it inflated itself like a double-breasted parachute and came to a rest on the old man's pipe. Great hoots of laughter filtered the between, and fearing it might end too soon, the old man unhooked the bra from the bowl of his pipe and, slipping it over his shoulders, made a series of light hops and skips in a burlesque jig, concluding with a rub of his crotch. To be sure, any excuse would have sufficed. Steen could not help but contribute a smile, not so much at the antics themselves but rather at the creature called MAN who performed them. However, his mind was uneasy over the fact that it now seemed that the lady was surely moving out, or how explain these two comedians, the clothes and their transportation?

He moved closer to the window and eased out the latch in an attempt to overhear something which might convince him of the contrary. At last the laughter ceased and the man with the cap loaded the clothes into the van. He mentioned something to the man with the pipe but it came over muffled and Steen could not make out the words. Again the intent must have been jocular, for the old man piped up jeering and made a pinch at his bra-bedecked chest. Then slipping the shells from his shoulders he sniffed, smiled, sniffed again, and tossed the garment in the air. Heartily blowing the cinders from his burner, he joined the man with the cap and together, one rubbing, one scratching, they disappeared inside.

It was a few moments before they appeared before the window. Temporarily Steen took the man with – now without – a cap for a woman, for he had exchanged headgear, now wearing on his head a ladies' wig. This the old man whipped from his skull with a poor pirouette before vanishing out of view, only to return with a similar whirl with his arm around the waist of a lady. *The* lady! Stunned, Steen pushed forward, quite unaware that the nature of his curiosity was nearing the crest of danger, his hands and face well whitened against the pane. There was no disputing it was she. There was the dark hair. The blue gown. The old man held her close, the pair of them circling and circling. Finally they disappeared. All the while the capless fool continued to laugh hysterically. Steen turned his eyes from the scene, unbelieving, and looked deep into the dark pool of his untouched coffee. Quite rightly his reflection, too, shook its head in disbelief. That the house was, or had been, a haven of ill repute, Steen had never envisaged. Certainly the collection of clothes did nothing to contend with the notion. Nevertheless, he felt he was perhaps being a trifle too presumptuous. Imagine! Instead he considered the lighter option, that the lady had merely begun to sing a little ditty and the old man, not to miss out on the chance, had responded with the idea of a dance. All very harmless. The capless fool had now followed suit and there was no one before the pane.

For some while he remained before the window, resisting the urge to leave it. The sun was playing peekaboo; beyond, a siren whirred. Beneath, in the yard, a feline yob boxed with its mitts the bedraggled bra. Steen made to return the latch to the frame when suddenly, from the door below, the old man's backside appeared. His feet shuffled outwards, then shuffled inwards, out once more, inwards. So that he was no sooner visible than he was invisible again. Now he emerged fully, but sideways, his front turned from view. He was carrying something concealed from the eye of Steen, which no longer behind his window, was outside it, swollen in rapt attention. With a final gasping stretch his great strainings bore their fruit: a trace of hair, dark! A hint of blue, the gown! And now the man, happily reinstated with his cap, followed through.

Inflamed, Steen steadied his knees on the window ledge and cocked his head and a considerable part of his shoulders, a good bust's worth, out the window, as far as was possible without toppling to his death, the better to confirm his theory. The theory varnishing thus: that these two scoundrels, during their brief interim from candid camera, motivated by the handling and other sensual wonderments of lingerie, had allowed Old Father Instinct to apply the upper hand on Lady Reason and, so doing, feathered by the thought of fornication, had taken this pure innocent without her consent, and by the force of the brute, had exhausted her, possibly beaten her or worse. This noble bubble, the culmination of so many little stirrings, was soon to be burst, shot through, by a lance of impeccable bluntness.

A wild vociferation rang through the air. Steen, like a man possessed, was now toying with that aforementioned expiry, but naught but the last line could stop him now. The two men glanced over their shoulders, fish eyes searching for the essence of the cries. Who? What? Where? All manner of profanities were vying for their ears. At last at their wits' end they tossed the cursed dummy to the ground, dislodging a limb in the process, and swinging round their heads in perfect harmony sought out the culprit up in arms. Steen, for his part, fell suddenly silent. His jaw dropped. His nostrils flared. Two piebald saucers spun in their sockets. Strings of saliva suspended from his teeth. A mannequin!

To the yodel of Yahweh the old man looked up, the threads of initiative not all yet lost, and spying the figure by the window above made to roar a retaliation, but sight of the face and the expression thereon curtailed his words to a whisper, and with the majestic sweep of a magician's hand he blessed himself profusely.

The man with the cap, now gathering the thread, looked up to the window and back to his pal, up to the window and back to his pal. Temple tapped and turned askew. The one then looked to the other. In silence shook their heads. It was unanimous. A madman!

MOLLY McCLOSKEY

Hatteras

He used to read the paper from back to front and tease me about
the war. The big one. WW III.

'I feel sorry for you,' he said, 'I do. No caps in the air in Times
Square. No little flower heads hanging out of gun barrels. What
you have to look forward to,' he said, 'is a war without photo ops.
Without music or movies or old injuries that act up when it rains.
Just *prcow* . . . nothing.'

His hands rose in the shape of a column, blossomed into a
mushroom cloud.

'And what about you?' I said. 'Where will you be?'

'Oh I'll be there,' he said. 'I wouldn't miss it for the world.'

'So to speak.'

'I'll be there all right. But it'll be your night out.'

As regards the paper, he had his reasons.

'You go in the intended order,' he said, 'it's like some kinda
lousy joke. You've got your death squads, your dictator-
ships, your out-and-out lies. You've got some sixteen-year-old
from Charlotte knifing some fourteen-year-old from Mint Hill.
A drug deal *gone wrong*, it says. As if up to then it had been
such a nice idea. Ah . . . but look . . . *Paper Moon* is playing at
the Westgate. *The Way We Were*'s at the Met. The Mets are at
Shea. But by that time, you don't want to know about true love
or a no-hitter. You end up sneaking them, like *they're* the dirty
parts.'

*

Bill had always seemed old to me. At fourteen, at eighteen, twenty-six and dying. Though we were only eight years apart, it struck us both as generations. For someone so young, Bill had an acutely developed sense of nostalgia, and he took the passage of time personally. He'd come of age in an era when people were fast losing faith. He used to stalk around the house with his fingers raised in Vs of victory, his jowls shaking like a horse's.

'I am not a crook,' he'd burble.

Bill reckoned that line about summed it up. It wasn't like it was the first lie ever told, or even the biggest. Hardly the most interesting. But it was the one people didn't believe. And because I came of age in the aftermath of that particular mess and took things like napalm for granted, I offended him. I reminded him that life just went on, no matter what you learned. He harboured a very gentle, very prescient grudge against me, implicating me in future misdeeds, so that it became *my* war, *my* world gone wrong, *my* rot setting in.

What Bill believed was that at a certain point, perhaps just prior to the criminalisation of LSD, time should've stopped. Maybe it should've stopped that night in '71 when he put the big clumsy headphones on me and turned up the volume. This brave new world opening up inside my head as I watched Bill moving like a mime in front of me. Maybe it should've stopped in the middle of one of those races across the sandflats in Carolina, the two of us dead in our tracks at the fifty-yard line, frozen as a couple of relics from an unearthed Pompeii. But if it were up to me, I'd rather it stopped at Hatteras.

Hatteras is the name given to the cape, the inlet, the island itself. All part of a long, loose thread of land hanging down along the coast of Carolina. The eye of the needle – where the promontory meets the mainland – just over the border, in Virginia. East of Hatteras is the Atlantic, and west, the Pamlico Sound. If you keep south along the coast, you'll eventually hit Cape Fear;

north would bring you through Kitty Hawk. We used to summer somewhere in between.

Bill was sixteen and I was eight the first time he drove me out to Hatteras. The Sound side was calm, the moon three-quarters full, and when a breeze rose, the water rippled silver, as though a school of fish passed just under the surface. We lay flat on our backs on the sand, Bill talking about the stars.

'Billions and billions of them,' he said.

He said it just like Carl Sagan did on the TV on Sunday nights. Astronomy for the earthbound. Bill held his palm flat, face up, and moved it in a slow arc from left to right. His hand like a comet passing across the sky.

He wanted to be an astronomer. That he could live up there among the stars, just by being on a hilltop. He figured that'd be about the nicest office a body could ask for. Later, it was a pilot. Twin engines only. He'd run sorties down in Central America, but not for our government.

'I know what's what,' he'd say. 'I know whose side I'm on.'

Then he just wanted to be a nomad. Just to go somewhere. Anywhere. Roaming the docks in a short pea jacket. Like Brando on the waterfront. Doing the right thing.

It took him a few years – winters at the university earning some patently practical degree, summers manning jack hammers to shake the gibberish loose from his head – but he did go. To the Gold Coast. The Gulf of Mexico. The Bay of Biscay. Prince William Sound. Down to Honduras, where there were stars in the water. Bill figured he'd up and gone to heaven.

Dinoflagellates, they were called, but Bill said you couldn't put a name on a thing like that. You'd plunge your fist into the water and sparks would ignite. Scoop it up into your hand and watch all these silver lights shimmying down your arm or your oar.

I can see him tracing stars in a thousand places. Black nights with his back flat against some strange stone. Skies with no muck in them. He said lying on the ground, it was like the earth itself had held him in her arms. The way he felt small, but safe. You'd think feeling so small had to be better in exotic places. But it always came down to Hatteras. As geography goes, she was Bill's baby.

He came back to it when the sickness started.

I was seventeen by that time, older than Bill was when he first drove me to the Cape. I saw the change in him straight away. He'd lost weight, which wasn't unusual. The weight used to come and go, just as Bill did. But this time, the gauntness was in his eyes, too. Whatever it was that was eating away at him from the inside made him look at me hungrily. I felt sometimes as though he were behind bars in one of those dusty places, and I an emissary from the free world. I could bring him things from the outside. I could tell him: Keep the faith. That we were making progress on his case, that it wouldn't be long now. I could even touch him. But I could also come and go in a way he couldn't any more. And given the chance, I'd never take his place, nor offer him mine. Bill was dying and we both knew it.

The diagnosis was quick. There was never any mystery about the cancer. There were moments he sounded like his old self, and he said once that at least he should've gotten to choose.

'This off-the-shelf bullshit,' he called it.

Not even the doctor found it particularly interesting. Tragic, yes. But interesting? No. Bill had wanted to do something big in his life, something memorable, and now there was no time. So what he wished for was an extraordinary death. Something to baffle the pundits. But he was dying in a perfectly textbook fashion.

'I am a well-behaved statistic,' he said. 'And I come when I'm called.'

But there were times, too, in the beginning, when he refused to believe it. Or believe he couldn't beat it. When he maintained he was going to live a very long life because God was having so much fun fucking with him.

Later, he said: 'Looks like I was wrong.'

Either there was no God, or fucking with Bill wasn't all it was cracked up to be.

I hated the black humour. More than I hated the way his skin grew waxy, or his thick arms wispy. I hated it when he said: 'I always wanted to go places, but this is ridiculous.'

One day I came home and found him crying. He was lying perfectly still in the bed, staring at the white ceiling, tears sliding out of the corners of his eyes in neatly timed intervals. He raised his forearms gently off the bed; his fingers formed Vs.

'I am not a crook,' he said.

In a way, he looked relieved, lying there crying. He didn't care any more if I saw him, or if I saw he was scared. He was still drawing from the same well of smart-assed jokes, but the edge had gone off them. We started talking then, differently from before. Sometimes, strangely enough, about the future. I looked forward to him again, and after that, every day when school got out I'd go and sit with him, at home or in the hospital. We'd watch afternoon TV. *Lucy* or *Let's Make a Deal* or *Star Trek*. Bill was one of the original Trekkies and he knew all the lines. But he threw his own shapes on them.

'Beam me up, Scottie,' he'd say, 'but not so fucking fast.'

He reckoned the chemo was like being energised. Broken up into bits so that for split seconds you don't exist any more. Your cells all zapped. Then you find yourself back in one piece, lying in some strange bed, surrounded by people who may as well be from another planet. Queer knobs on their heads and looking down at you like you're just in from another dimension.

He used to ask me those afternoons what I'd be when I got out of school. I told him lots of different stories. It was a game we played. Everything from mafia moll to donut delivery girl. Bumping down the streets at dawn in a little white van. Glazed and chocolates twined like a linked chain across the back door. My name written in sugared twists along the side. Making people's mornings.

Sometimes it seemed wrong that he'd want to think about the future at all, when it didn't include him. But Bill had that odd relationship with time, and now, a kind of inside-out nostalgia was taking hold. He wanted to know what he'd miss, so that he could miss it while he had the chance. And he longed, wistfully, for things that had not yet happened.

One day he said, 'What about a tightrope walker?'

'Scared of heights,' I said. 'You know that.'

'Yeah. Luckily, I'm not. Could be a problem where I'm going.'

Those oblique references to heaven. He wondered could you see the stars from there, being so high up and all. Would they be at your feet then, could you hopscotch them Hollywood Boulevard-style. Or hold them in your hands.

But most likely, he said, it was a moot point.

By that time, I'd begun to dream about his death. Off-white dreams, just an atmosphere, really, of absence. Less about his death than about him dead. Nothing as plain as a place at the table or an empty bed. But flat landscapes, horizons I couldn't trust, silences in which I heard voices, as though I were too long in solitary and losing it.

I'd go to him in the mornings before heading off to school. Leave him something – some juice or a note or a drawing. He was always asleep. Dreams of his own I never asked about. The last thing I wanted to know was what went on in his head when he had no say in the matter. But I used to feel I'd betrayed him with my snow-white skies, my stretches of desert. As though I were trying on his death for size, creating spaces that contained no trace of him. Preparing for the day, maybe only months from now, when I'd suddenly think of him, and realise I hadn't thought of him for hours.

But back then, I saw Bill everywhere, and everything I saw, no matter how tenuous the connection, brought me back to him. Arriving at school those mornings, the cars in the parking lot. Their engines just switched off, but still creaking in the cold. Bill in bed, not able to move, but with life in him still. Times I wanted to kick him, or curse at him, like you would a machine that had quit on you. No logic. Just the relief of having acted, of having not just sat there stymied. Times he knew I was angry with him, and the way that seemed to lift him. If I was angry with him, that meant he must be doing something. And doing something meant being alive. Anything but pity. Pity was like a line I drew in the sand. But anger was a circle we could stand inside.

And then the good days. That spring there were still a few. Taking him for drives, like he used to me. Wheeling him down the sidewalks in the chair, when he wasn't able to walk. Out to Reynolda Gardens, where you could catch a whiff of tobacco from the cigarette factory. Green lawns and the white dogwoods and wafting over us, if the wind was right, the faint smell of death in the air.

We'd stop the chair under a certain willow tree. Bill would lean his head back and close his eyes and I'd ask him questions, safe ones, ones I knew the answers to.

'What do you see,' I'd ask, 'when you close your eyes?'

'Stars,' he'd say quickly. It was a rehearsed routine of ours.

'Many?'

A smile would push at the corners of his mouth, just enough for me to see.

'Billions,' he'd say.

Where he most wanted to go, of course, was out to Hatteras. And we promised him we would. When school finished, the four

of us would pack up the car and Bill and I would leave Mom and
Dad at the rental place and I'd drive out to the slip at night-time.
Just the two of us. The ring of lights winking from the shoreline.
All the lights above us. Bill not having to close his eyes.

It won't be long now, we told him.

'Soon,' I said.

Nights, that May, I lay beside him in the back yard, and listened
to him recite the constellations. Or he'd be propped up on the
blanket I'd spread -- he was so thin then I could lift him -- and I'd
follow his finger to where it pointed towards a planet. I didn't say
that I saw the spaces between things now, rather than the things
themselves. That I thought about my life with him not in it,
rather than about him sitting there beside me. But he knew. He
must've known.

Bill's dying. I'm finishing high school, this very night. There are
things going to happen he'll never see. I want to stand up, place
my square cap over my heart and make a fiery, inspirational
speech. Assuring him that, despite the many dire predictions,
certain horrors will never come to pass. That there's a chance the
course of history still can be diverted, that power can be
harnessed for the good. Because I can't see Bill, but I can feel
him. His face is there among the sea of faces. And what it feels like
now is that he's behind me, only just coming up in the world. It's
all ahead of you, I want to say, and it's not all bad. Believe me.

Then I see him, and in an instant everything changes. He's
sitting in the back row, apart from my mother and father for some
reason. He's wearing a black jacket and sunglasses. Only his head
moves. He keeps his arms crossed over his chest and looks slowly
from side to side, casing the crowd. Like he's the secret service at
some big political do and I'm the one running for office. Who's
taking care of whom here?

He disappears again. His head behind the person in front of

him. And I sink lower in my chair, so that I'm there beside him. I can whisper it in his ear then, all these things I know. About how the world, with its perils, is just a place he's read about in books. One of those books you stumble on before you're old enough to understand, so that for days after, until you work up the courage to ask, you think that locusts might swarm over your back yard, or killer bees. That big holes in the sky are opening up, plates in the earth shifting to a dangerous degree, toxins rife in the countryside, deadlier than anything you can see, or feel.

I could tell Bill the truth, as I knew it. About the spaces between things, the non-events. I could tell him that his name won't be buried in the obits, in small print, smaller than the movie listings, smaller even than the Mets. That for once, we could do things in their proper order. We'd start with the funnies, then baseball under the lights. All the junk he could eat. I'd tell him that the dirty parts were just freaks of nature, things that never really came to pass. Not in his lifetime, anyway, and not where we lived. I'd tell him that those whispers in the doctor's office were just that: whispers. That it wouldn't be long now before he felt the sandflats beneath his heels, the grains more plentiful than cells, softer than anything he's ever felt. I'd tell him that come summer, we'd cross the sound near Cape Lookout, up along Raleigh Bay, past Portsmouth, through Ocracoke and on into Hatteras. That there are a thousand skies still to come.

GILLMAN NOONAN

Roles

As usual, they strolled through the small park on their way home. The wind had a sudden edge, finally joining the winter camp. Leaves swirled in the air, and George pretended to jump for them but Danny ignored the world around. Miss McCarthy at nursery school had told him that in the Chinese year he was a monkey.

'We all know you're a monkey,' George joked.

'I don't want to be!'

At the door now, Danny holding back the tears.

'I bet you wouldn't want to be me,' George said. 'In the Chinese calendar I'm an ox.'

'I don't care!'

They took the hateful thing into the front room, dried the tears that flowed, talked cleverly of ringing up the Chinese Embassy to arrange honorary membership of the monkey sign, switched on a children's programme, and forgot about it.

George washed up in the kitchen. A leaf had stuck to the window and was slowly slipping down like a large brown slug. Curiously the pictures that came to him of fallen leaves were of life beginning, love in the clasp of hands as leaves were kicked, the tenderest pink of skin when the baby came amidst the swirl of leaves in Merrion Square where he paced like the proverbial expectant father, before racing around again to Hollis Street hospital. And that night he thought they might have made the child, the night Kate and himself, waiting for a bus, got a lift back to Dun Laoghaire from a surgeon seeking human contact after a day of amputation. A total stranger to them, he talked compulsively about himself while leaves caught in his wipers, now whipped forever across the mind's recall.

'Yes, Mummy will be home soon.'

Tension mounted in George as the afternoon wore on. By now it was like an old friend that sat with him on the couch. He knew its every twitch. And there she was back from her office and looking pale but with that briskness of movement that now so unnerved him. Their rhythms had changed. He followed the new one with almost clinical interest: first a 'quick pee', then the picking up of Danny's toys, of Danny himself for a 'quick scrub', the rattling and clinking of things in the kitchen that he had washed up and put away in their usual place, the screech of hangers sliding on the bar in the bedroom wardrobe. Why did she always end *there*?

He knew what it was for her, a noisy affirmation of will, a way of saying that now she was back and though exhausted from her day she was ready to take over the management of the boy and the home and he, George, could slide off into his room and continue his translation work. Or smoke his pipe and pretend to work, sprawled on his old leather settee, where she had more than once surprised him.

He worked, a translation of a new do-it-yourself book on papermaking. The heavy words of the introduction, the fibres' molecular attraction, their colloidal properties, the pretence of all words weighed on him, as though the mind knew how it could master such tricks and yearned to return to the clouded centre of things which was life's slow drift through time, its shaping and dissolving of love. The past, like stars, had its quiet magic. You didn't gape at the stars in constant wonder but at moments they amazed because you were alive to see them, as the past amazed because it was yours alone. Gudrun in Germany, Marie-Claire in

Paris, a few others when bedding them in those unterrified years was part of a linguistic adventure, snuggling down with wine and cigarettes into the unfamiliar idiom, an earthy phrase from some Bavarian farmyard, a thrust like a rapier from a Paris alley. A switchback railway fell on Gudrun. No luck for George at that fairground. And Marie-Claire found a rich American doubtless more fun than George and plonk and the tiresome way he seemed determined to master the idiomatically correct orgasm.

George's mother died and he bought a small house with the money she left him. When he met Kate he was making a living but nothing more and he warned her, when she moved in with him, that his 'at first glance laid-back existence' was deceptive. There was nothing interesting in it. He was a rather fusty housebound fellow, bookish, indolent, slightly overweight, and at forty-one possibly into his romantic dotage. She brushed aside all his silly words. Sex with Kate was natural, unidiomatic, even inarticulate, like brewing up strong sweet tea. When at his age he was beginning to think that it would become a functional, even furtive, businesss she led him out into the sunlight where things just happened. On a visit home to her parents in Cork she realised that she loved him. On her return to Dublin she realised that she was pregnant.

Well, he'd had a good look at that one. George, fastidious translator, was intrigued by the choice of words. When does one actually 'realise'? What was it? Was it, like a quick pee, felt in the mind or in the body? Had she stood by the Lough in Cork, watching the sun burning in the windows of the houses, and 'realised' love? Can a woman 'realise' she is pregnant, or does she simply count the days she is overdue?

He'd had a good look and bought the whole caboodle. They were tender and loving, that was more important than words. He threw himself into wedding arrangements, puffing his pipe like an old engine that had discovered unsuspected fire in its belly. The drama of fatherhood waited to be written by his hand alone. Kate returned to work soon after Danny was born. A childminder was found so that George could work as usual. The same routine was still in operation except that Danny now spent half the day at nursery.

Nothing had gone wrong, as far as George could see, except that routines were dull. The drama of fatherhood was still at the prologue stage, and but fitfully inspired. He was older and fustier and only waited to slip crablike into his lair, and Kate was older, strands of grey showing in her hair which she made no attempt to hide. Their love life was still vigorous but rather with the energy required for the weekly bulk shopping. They had ceased to talk about much else beyond the familiar coping – as now in the front room, eating the lasagna Kate had prepared the night before, saying things but really watching the news, *Danny sit up, Danny get down, Danny will you for the luvagod* . . .

Still, Kate came in from work and bashed things around as if she at least *expected* something more of the approaching evening. But with Danny tucked up, a documentary showing, union steward's work to hand or another book on food and health (no novels now for Kate), whatever signal she may have given had snuffed itself out, or dried up in the crackle of paper, or simply looked at itself in the bathroom mirror and yawned. Until George rose at last to say, as if it were the first time such a notion occurred to him, 'I think I'll stroll down for a pint.' Adding, depending on his mood, 'Want anything? Diet peanuts? Additive-free crisps?'

Pausing inside the door of the pub, George, connoisseur of pipe smoke and related smells, flared his nostrils to capture the evening's particular blend. It was distinctly autumnal, with a base of damp brought in on the coats piled around the pool table.

'The usual, George?'

'Please, Harry.'

He filled his pipe, savouring the thought of smoking it among people and not out of doors or in the exile of his den. Most of the pool players were known to him by their first names and he in time had been accepted by them, still an outsider but one who in his taciturn way had slotted himself in between their loyalties. Bob and Maureen were there, back from their honeymoon. Watching Maureen, her slim figure at that curious angle to the cue that some women adopted, suggesting that even when their breasts were small like hers they still expected them to get in the way, George's mood darkened. He took a sip of stout and sucked the cream off his moustache. Maureen would change too. Look at her, laughing as if pubs and pool were perennials of life. Was it only self-centred old buzzards like himself could walk into a pub with much the same attitudes they'd had twenty years before? Perhaps Kate had woken up to this. Having affectionately accepted his own version of himself as a fossilised romantic, had she woken up one day to the truth of it?

It was then that George, breaking off, watching the balls scatter, a stripe, a solid, falling in, choice of either, saw a thought like a dark rider just out of vision but coming up fast as he bent over his cue taking a stripe into the centre bag, stunning back for another into the bottom right. The rider galloped past shouting his message that hung in the air and settled like dust around the baffled man.

Kate had taken a lover!

She must have! (George chalked his cue as if intent on wearing away the tip.) Why else should she stop reading fiction? You only did that when your life became one! All those 'endless' union meetings! And now George was sure it was Kate he had seen walking with a man on Sandymount Strand that day he drove down the coast road to deliver some work to an agency. It had looked like Kate's figure in her red coat far out near the bait diggers with their buckets, and now he knew it had been!

'You're on stripes, George.'

'So I am. Silly of me. Two shots to you, Bill.'

The wind had dropped and a mist had come in from the bay, falling like a ghostly veil upon the night. The house was in darkness. There was snooker on the television. If he kept the sound down he might watch for a while over a last can of stout from the fridge. He switched on the set, killing the sound but not before a brief burst of applause ripped through the silent house.

The door opened at his back. In the flickering light she looked old standing there in her nightgown, a granny, her hair wild.

'I'm pregnant,' she said. 'But I don't think I want another baby.' She walked past him to sit on the bench he had fashioned beneath the small bay window. He caught a faint whiff of her perfume that touched in him a sense of her vulnerability, a small prop she needed. Even in the way she sat now watching him, the strength of her silence was a clue to the will she would have to show, the manageress facing down the opposition. He lit his pipe with the feeling of taking a liberty in the room. It crystallised his mood. He was on sufferance. She would dictate the pace and he would respond.

'Is it by that man I saw you walking with on Sandymount Strand?'

'What?'

'I saw you with him. I was just driving past. Not spying or anything, you know.'

'Jack Slater? Are you serious?'

'Was that Jack? Well, why not? He's . . . charming. And we haven't exactly been . . .'

'No, we haven't exactly been. So what's strange about that?'

'There was nothing?'

'You're a fool. Joan Slater is my friend.'

'Why . . . ?'

'I confided in Jack.'

'Not in your husband?'

'I knew what he would say. I know what he'll say now.'

From the street the light was lunar, pitting each face in the other's cold radiance. The baize on the screen was like a memory of green, how the world had looked. This was their special light, the way it had been when they had lain down in this room to engender a boy. But Danny had floated in with no hint of rejection. This new life was not so lucky. It had stopped at the trading post where a man and a woman sat in the semi-darkness of their life together.

'You think,' he began, 'that I would want you to have the child although it would mean . . .'

'Yes, although it would mean sacrificing yourself while I got on with my career and kept the car on the road, driving into work each morning to my nice clean office.'

'How do you know . . . ?'

'I know you. You're a softie. Which is fine. You would want to do it all yourself. Without a hint of role strain. Oh no, that's for the magazines. But I don't want to live with a sacrificial softie of a man. I mean, it's bad enough now, isn't it? We're managing but with . . . with gritted teeth.'

'We're par for the course, I should imagine nowadays.'

'The child would be born with a price tag . . . which you would magnanimously pay. I don't want that.'

'It offends your sense of honest accounting.'

'You can find any words you like for it.'

'So even if I said we could find a child minder and . . .'

'It was just going off that stupid pill. Don't you understand? It was an accident.'

'Like Danny?'

Amazed, he saw her eyes glitter, a tear slipping down her cheek. It was as if a small silvery snail had emerged from a crack in the statue. He wanted to rise and sit by her but his thoughts were cold.

'Danny was different,' she said at last.

'It's my child too.'

'Yes, of course. But is that the point?'

'For me it is. How could it not be?'

All of a sudden the television went dead. The room was plunged into darkness, and they saw that all the lights in the street had gone out. In the dark they still stared at each other, and George knew then that the words he had spoken were precisely the ones she, from her own dark side of life, had wanted. Each depended on the other for persuasion.

'Danny says Miss McCarthy said he was a monkey in the Chinese year.'

'I know. He told me all about it. He said you would ring the Chinese Embassy tomorrow.'

'I must get him something.'

She turned to the street and for an instant, just before the lights came on again, she saw him clearly, the monkey, crouched in a tree. He shone with life, silvery, his eyes like points of fierce vision in the dark, hugging his young, hardly aware of it.

WILLIAM TREVOR

An Evening Out

In the theatre bar they still talked, not hurrying over their drinks although an announcement had warned that the performance would begin in two minutes. There were more people in the bar than it could comfortably accommodate, crushed close against the bar itself and in the corners, some just beginning to make their way through the several doorways to the auditorium.

'The performance will begin in one minute,' the peremptory Tannoy voice reminded, and quite suddenly the bar was almost empty.

The barman was a character, gloomy-faced, skin and bone, bespectacled; lank like old string, he said himself. The barmaid was younger by quite a bit, and cheerfully plump.

'Oh, look,' she said. 'That woman.'

One woman had not left with the others and showed no sign of doing so. She was in a corner, sitting at one of the few tables the bar provided. All around her, on the shelf that ran around the walls, on the seats of chairs, there were empty glasses. Her own was three-quarters full of gin and tonic.

'Deaf, d'you think?' the barman wondered, and the barmaid remarked that the theatre was never a place for the hard of hearing, it stood to reason. It could be of course that a deaf-aid had been temporarily turned off and then forgotten.

The woman they spoke of was smartly dressed, two shades of green; a coat that was tweed on one side and waterproof on the other was draped over the other chair at her table. The remains of beauty strikingly lit her features, seeming to be less casually, less incidentally, there than it might have been earlier in her life. Touches of grey were allowed in her fair hair, adding a distinction that went with the other changes time had wrought.

'Excuse me, madam,' the barman said, 'but the performance has begun.'

What a city London is! Jeffrey thought, staring up at the dark bronze features of Sir Henry Havelock beneath the sprinkling of pigeon droppings that lightened the soldier's crown. The last of an April twilight was slipping away, the city at its best, as it also was – in Jeffrey's view – when dawn was turning into day. In Trafalgar Square the traffic was clogged, a crawl of lumbering red buses and patient taxis, a cyclist now and again weaving through. People gathered at the crossing lights, seeming to lose something of themselves in each small multitude as obediently they waited to move forward when the signal came. Pigeons swooped above territory they claimed as theirs, and landed on it to waddle after titbits, or snapped at one another, flapping away together into the sky, still in dispute.

Jeffrey turned away from it all, from Sir Henry Havelock and the pigeons and the four great lions, the floodlights just turned on, illuminating the façade of the National Gallery. 'Won't do to keep her waiting,' he murmured, causing two girls who were passing to snigger. He kept her waiting longer, for when he reached it he entered the Salisbury in St Martin's Lane and ordered a Bell's, and then called out that it had better be a double.

He needed it. Truth to tell, he needed a second but he shook away the thought, reprimanding himself: neither of them would get anywhere if he was tipsy. On the street again he searched the pockets of his mackintosh for the little plastic container that was rattling somewhere, and when he found it in his jacket he took two of his breath fresheners.

*

Evelyn drew back slightly from the barman's elderly, untidy face, from cheeks that fell into hollows, false teeth. He said again that the performance had begun.

'Thank you,' she said. 'Actually, I'm waiting for someone.'

'We could send your friend in if you liked to go on ahead. If you have your ticket. They're sometimes not particular about a disturbance before a play's got going.'

'No, actually we're just meeting here. We're not going to the theatre.'

She read, behind heavily-rimmed lenses, bewilderment in the man's eyes. It was unusual, she read next, the thought flitting through his confusion. He settled for that, a conclusion reached.

'You didn't mind my asking? Only I said to my colleague, where's the need for both of them to be late if they have their tickets on them?'

'It's very kind of you.'

'Thank you, madam.'

Near to where she sat he cleared the shelf of glasses, wiped it down with a damp grey cloth, moved on, expertly balancing the further glasses he collected. 'Lady's waiting for her friend,' he said to the barmaid, who was washing up at a sink behind the bar. 'They're not attending the show tonight.'

Evelyn was aware of the glances from behind the bar. Speculation would come later, understandable when there was time to kill. For the moment she was no more than a woman on her own.

'D'you think I could have another?' she called out, suddenly deciding to. 'When you have a minute?'

She speculated herself then, wondering about whoever was destined to walk in. Oh, Lord! so often she had thought when an unsuitable arrival had abruptly brought such wondering to an end. 'Oh no,' she had even murmured to herself, looking away in a futile pretence that she was expecting no one. Doggedly they'd always come – the Lloyd's bank manager, the choral-music enthusiast, the retired naval officer who turned out to be a cabin steward, the widowed professor who'd apologised and gone away, the one who made up board games. Even before they spoke their doggedness and their smiles appeared to cover a multitude of sins.

She had all her life been obsessively early for appointments, and waiting yet again she made a resolution: this time if it was no good there wouldn't be a repetition. She'd just leave it; though of course a disappointment, it might be a relief.

Her drink came. The barman didn't linger. She shook her head when he said he'd bring her change.

'That's very kind of you, madam.'

She smiled that away, and was still smiling when a man appeared in the open doorway. He was hesitant, looking about him as if the place were crowded and there were several women to choose from, his nervousness not disguised. When he came closer he nodded before he spoke.

'Jeffrey,' he said. 'Evie?'

'Well, Evelyn actually.'

'Oh, I'm awfully sorry.'

His mackintosh was worn in places but wasn't grubby. His high cheekbones stood out, the skin tight where they stretched it. He didn't look at all well nourished. His dark hair, not a fleck of grey in it, was limp and she wondered if perhaps he was recovering from flu.

'Would you like your drink topped up?' he offered in a gentlemanly way. 'Nuts? Crisps?'

'No, I'm happy, thanks.'

He was fastidious, you could tell. Was there a certain vulnerability beneath that edgy manner? She always stipulated well-spoken, and on that he could not be faulted. If he was recovering from even a heavy cold, he'd naturally look peaky; no one could help that. He took off his mackintosh and a blue muffler, revealing a tweed jacket that almost matched the pale brown of his corduroy trousers.

'My choice of rendezvous surprise you?' he said.

'Perhaps a little.'

It didn't now that she had met him, for there was something about him that suggested he thought things out: theatre bars were empty places when a performance was on; there wouldn't be the embarrassment of approaches made by either of them to the wrong person. He didn't say that, but she knew. Belatedly he apologised for keeping her waiting.

'It doesn't matter in the least.'

'You're sure I can't bring you another drink?'

'No, really, thank you.'

'Well, I'll just get something for myself.'

At the bar Jeffrey asked about wine. 'D'you have white? Dry?'

'Indeed we do, sir.' The barman reached behind him and lifted a bottle from an ice bucket. 'Grinou,' he said. 'We like to keep it cool, being white.'

'Grinou?'

'It's what the wine's called, sir. La Combe de Grinou. The label's a bit washed away, but that's what it's called. Very popular in here, the Grinou is.'

Jeffrey took against the man, the way he often did with people serving him. He guessed that the barmaid looked after the man in a middle-aged daughterly way, listening to his elderly woes and ailments, occasionally inviting him to a Christmas celebration. Her daytime work was selling curtain material, Jeffrey surmised; the man had long ago retired from the same department store. Something like that it would be, the theatre bar their real world.

'All right, I'll try a glass,' he said.

*

They talked for a moment about the weather and then about the bar they were in, commenting on the destruction of its Georgian plasterwork, no more than a corner of the original ceiling remaining. From time to time applause or laughter reached them from the theatre's auditorium. Gingerly in their conversation they moved on to more personal matters.

Forty-seven they'd said he was. *Photographer*, they'd given as his profession on the personal details' sheet, and she had thought of the photographers you saw on television, a scrum of them outside a celebrity's house or pushing in at the scene of a crime. But on the phone the girl had been reassuring: a newspaper photographer wasn't what was meant. 'No, not at all like that,' the girl had said. 'Nor weddings neither.' Distinguished in his field, the girl had said; there was a difference.

She tried to think of the names of great photographers and could remember only Cartier-Bresson, without a single image coming into her mind. She wondered about asking what kind of camera he liked best, but asked instead what kind of photographs he took.

'Townscapes,' he said. 'Really only townscapes.'

She nodded confidently, as if she caught the significance of that, as if she appreciated the attraction of photographing towns.

'Parts of Islington,' he said. 'Those little back streets in Hoxton. People don't see what's there.'

His lifetime's project was to photograph London in all its idiosyncrasies. He mentioned places: Hungerford Bridge, Drummond Street, Worship Street, Brick Lane, Wellclose Square. He spoke of manhole covers and shadows thrown by television dishes, and rain on slated roofs.

'How very interesting,' she said.

What she sought was companionship. Sometimes when she made her way to the Downs or the coast she experienced the weight of solitude; often in the cinema or the theatre she would have liked to turn to someone else to say what she'd thought of this interpretation or that. She had no particular desire to be treated to candle-lit dinners, which the bureau – the Bryanston Square Introduction Bureau – had at first assumed would be a priority; but she would not have rejected such attentions, provided they came from an agreeable source. Marriage did not come into it, but nor was it entirely ruled out.

People she knew were not aware that she was a client at the Bryanston Square Bureau, not that she was ashamed of it. There would perhaps have been some surprise, but easily she could have weathered that. What was more difficult to come to terms with, and always had been, was the uneasy sense that the truth seemed to matter less than it should, both in the agency itself and in the encounters it provided. As honestly as she knew how, she had completed the personal details' sheet, carefully deliberating before she so much as marked, one way or the other, each little box, correctly recording her age, at present fifty-one; and when an encounter took place she was at pains not to allow mistaken impressions to go unchecked. But even so there was always that same uneasiness, the nagging awareness that falsity was natural in what she was engaged upon.

'You drive?' he asked.

He watched her nod, covering her surprise. It always took them aback, that question; he couldn't think why. She seemed quite capable, he thought, and tried to remember what it said on the information he'd been sent. Had she been involved with a language school? Something like that came back to him and he mentioned it.

'That was a while ago,' she said.

She was alone now; and, as Jeffrey understood it, devoted some of her time to charity work; he deduced that there must be private means.

'My mother died in nineteen ninety-seven,' she said. 'I looked after her during her last years. A full-time occupation.'

Jeffrey imagined a legacy after the mother's death; the father, he presumed, had departed long before.

'I'm afraid photography is something I don't know much about,' she said, and he shrugged, vaguely indicating that that was only to be expected. A tooth ached a bit, the same one as the other night and coming on as suddenly, the last one on the right, at the bottom.

'You found it interesting,' he said, 'languages and that?'

She was more promising than the insurance woman, or the hospital sister they'd tried so hard to interest him in. He'd said no to both, but they'd pressed, the way they sometimes did. He'd been indifferent this time, but even so he'd agreed. While he prodded cautiously with his tongue he learnt that passing on a familiarity with foreign languages was, in fact, not a particularly interesting way of making a living. He wondered if the barman kept aspirin handy; more likely, though, the barmaid might have some; or the Gents might run to a dispenser.

'Excuse me a sec,' he said.

'Oh yes, there's something in the Gents,' the old barman said when the barmaid had poked about in her handbag and had shaken her head. 'Just inside the door, sir.'

But when Jeffrey put a pound in nothing came out. Too late he saw – scrawled on a length of perforated stamp paper and stuck too high to be noticed – *Out of Order*. He swore hotly. If the woman hadn't been there he'd have created a scene, demanding his pound back, even claiming he had put in two.

'You have a car?' he enquired quite bluntly when he returned to the theatre bar, because on the way back from the Gents it had occurred to him that she had only said she could drive. *Driver?* it enquired on the wretchedly long-winded personal data thing, but

he always asked, just to be sure. He was modest in his expectations where the Bryanston Square Introduction Bureau was
concerned. He sought no more than a car-owner who would
transport him and his photographic equipment from one chosen
area of London to another, someone who – as privately he put it
to himself – would be drawn into his work. He imagined a quiet
person, capable after instruction of unfolding and setting up a
tripod, of using a simple light-meter, of making notes and keeping
a record, who would enjoy becoming part of things. He imagined
conversations that were all to do with the enterprise he had
undertaken; nothing more was necessary. He naturally had not
revealed any of these details on the Bryanston Square application
form he had completed eighteen months ago, believing that it
would be unwise to do so.

'It's just I wondered,' he said in the theatre bar, 'if you possessed a car?'

He watched her shaking her head. She'd had a car until a year
ago, a Nissan. 'I hardly ever used it,' she explained. 'I really
didn't.'

He didn't let his crossness show, but disappointment felt like a
weight within him. It wearied him, as disappointment had a way
of doing. The nearest there'd ever been was the social worker
with the beaten-up Ford Escort, or ages before that the club
receptionist with the Mini. But neither had lasted long enough to
be of any real help and both had turned unpleasant in the end. All
that wasted effort, this time again; he might as well just walk
away, he thought.

'My turn to get us a drink,' she said, taking a purse from her
handbag and causing him to wonder if she had an aspirin in there
too.

He didn't ask. He'd thought as he set out that if yet again there
was nothing doing there might at least be the consolation of
dinner – which references to toothache could easily put the

kibosh on. He wondered now about L'Etape. He'd often paused to examine the menu by the door.

'Wine, this was.' He handed her his glass and watched her crossing the empty space to the bar. She wasn't badly dressed: no reason why she shouldn't be up to L'Etape's tariff.

She listened while he went through his cameras, giving the manufacturers' names, and details about flash and exposure. Nine, he had apparently, a few of them very old and better than any on the market now. His book about London had been commissioned and would run to almost a thousand pages.

'Gosh!' she murmured. Halfway through her third gin and tonic, she felt pleasantly warm, happy enough to be here although she knew by now that none of this was any good. 'Heavens, you'll be busy!' she said. His world was very different from hers, she added, knowing she must not go on about hers, that it would be tedious to mention all sorts of things. Why should anyone be interested in her rejection more than twenty years ago of someone she had loved? Why should anyone be interested in knowing that she had done so, it seemed now, for no good reason beyond the shadow of doubt there'd been? A stranger would not see the face that she still saw, or hear the voice she heard; or understand why, afterwards, she had wanted no one else; or hear what, afterwards, had seemed to be a truth – that doubt played tricks in love's confusion. And who could expect a stranger to want to hear about the circumstances of a mother's lingering illness and the mercy of her death in a suburban house? You put it all together and it made a life; you lived in its aftermath, but that, too, was best kept back. She smiled at her companion through these reflections, for there was no reason not to.

'I was wondering about L'Etape,' he said.

Imagining this to be another camera, she shook her head, and he said that L'Etape was a restaurant. It was difficult then, difficult to say that perhaps they should not begin something that could not be continued, which his manner suggested had been his conclusion also. They were not each other's kind: what at first had seemed to be a possibility hadn't seemed so after three-quarters of an hour, as so often was the way. So much was right: she would have liked to say so; she would have liked to say that she'd enjoyed their encounter and hoped he'd shared that with her. Her glass was nowhere near empty, nor was his; there was no hurry.

'But then I'd best get back,' she said. 'If you don't mind.'

She wondered if in his life too there had been a mistake that threw a shadow, if that was why he was looking around for someone to fill a gap he had never become used to. She smiled in case her moment of curiosity showed, covering it safely over.

'It was just a thought,' he said. 'L'Etape.'

The interval curtain came down at an emotional moment. There was applause, and then the first chattering voices reached the bar, which filled up quickly. The noise of broken conversation spread in the quiet it had disturbed, until the Tannoy announcement warned that three minutes only remained, then two, then one.

'I'm afraid we shut up shop now,' the elderly barman said and the plump barmaid hurried about, collecting the glasses and pushing the chairs against one wall so that the cleaners could get at the floor when they came in the morning. 'Sorry about that,' the barman apologised.

Jeffrey considered making a fuss, insisting on another drink, since the place after all was a public bar. He imagined himself waking up at two or three in the morning and finding himself depressed because of the way the evening had gone. He would remember then the stern features of Sir Henry Havelock in Trafalgar Square and the two girls giggling because he'd said something out loud. He would remember the *Out of Order* sign in the Gents. She should have been more explicit about the driving on that bloody form instead of wasting his time.

He thought of picking up a glass and throwing it at the upside-down bottles behind the bar, someone's leftover slice of lemon flying through the air, glass splintering into the ashtrays and the ice-bucket, all that extra for them to clear up. He thought of walking away without another word, leaving the woman to make her peace with the pair behind the bar. Ridiculous they were, ridiculous not to have an aspirin somewhere.

'It was brilliant, your theatre-bar idea,' she said as they passed through the foyer. The audience's laughter reached them, a single ripple, quietening at once. The box office was closed, a board propped up against its ornate brass bars. Outside, the posters for the play they hadn't seen wildly proclaimed its virtues.

'Well,' he said, though without finality; uncertain, as in other ways he had seemed to be.

Yet surely she hadn't been mistaken; surely he must have known also, and as soon as she had. She imagined him with one of his many cameras, skulking about the little streets of Hoxton. There was no reason why a photographer shouldn't have an artistic temperament, which would account for his nerviness or whatever it was.

'I don't suppose,' he said, 'you'd have an aspirin?'

He had a toothache. She searched her handbag, for she sometimes had paracetamol.

'I'm sorry,' she said, still rummaging.

'It doesn't matter.'

'It's bad?'

He said he would survive. 'I'll try the Gents in L'Etape. Sometimes there's a vending machine in a Gents.'

They fell into step. It wasn't why he'd suggested L'Etape, he said. 'It's just that I felt it would be nice,' he said. 'A regretful dinner.'

When they came to a corner, he pointed up a narrower, less crowded street than the one they'd walked along. 'It's there,' he said. 'That blue light.'

Feeling sorry for him, she changed her mind.

The hat-check girl brought paracetamol to their table, since there wasn't a vending machine in the Gents. Jeffrey thanked her, indicating with a gesture that he would tip her later. At a white grand piano a pianist in a plum-coloured jacket reached out occasionally for a concoction in a tall lemonade glass, not ceasing to play his Scott Joplin medley. A young French waiter brought menus and rolls. He made a recommendation but his English was incomprehensible. Jeffrey asked him to repeat what he'd said, but it was hopeless. Typical, that was, Jeffrey thought, ordering lamb, with peas and polenta.

'I'm sorry about your toothache,' she said.

'It'll go.'

The place was not quite full. Several tables, too close to the piano, were still unoccupied. Someone applauded when the pianist began a showy variation of 'Mountain Greenery'. He threw his head about as he played, blond hair flopping.

'Shall I order the wine?' Jeffrey offered. 'D'you mind?' He never said beforehand that he intended not to pay. Better just to let it happen, he always thought.

'No, of course I don't mind,' she said.

'That's kind of you.' He felt better than he had all evening, in spite of the nagging in his lower jaw and that, he knew, would lessen when the paracetamol got going. It was always much better when they said yes to a regretful dinner, when the disappointment began to slip away. 'We'll have the Château Lamothe,' he ordered. 'The '95.'

She was aware that a woman at a distant table, in a corner where there were potted plants, kept glancing at her. The woman was with two men and another woman. She seemed faintly familiar; so did one of the men.

'*Madame*,' the young waiter interrupted her efforts to place the couple, arriving with the escalope she'd ordered. '*Bon appétit, madame.*'

'Thank you.'

She liked the restaurant, the thirties' style, the pale blue lighting, the white grand piano, the aproned waiters. She liked her escalope when she tasted it, and the heavily buttered spinach, the little out-of-season new potatoes. She liked the wine.

'Not bad, this place,' her companion said. 'What d'you think?'

'It's lovely.'

They talked more easily than they had in the theatre bar and it was the theatre bar they spoke about, since it was their common ground. Odd, they'd agreed, that old barman had been; odd, too, that 'barmaid' should still be a common expression, implying in this case someone much younger, the word hanging on from another age.

'Oh, really . . .' she began when a second bottle of wine was suggested, and then she thought, why not? They talked about the Bryanston Square Bureau, which was common ground too.

'They muddle things up,' he said. 'They muddle people up. They get them wrong, with all their little boxes and their question-naires.'

'Yes, perhaps they do.'

The woman who'd kept glancing across the restaurant was

listening to one of the men, who appeared to be telling a story. There was laughter when he finished. The second man lit a cigarette.

'Heavens!' Evelyn exclaimed, although she hadn't meant to.

Jeffrey turned to look and saw, several tables away, four smartly dressed people, one of the two women in a striped black and scarlet dress, the other with glasses, her pale blonde hair piled elaborately high. The men were darkly suited. Like people in an advertisement, he thought, an impression heightened by the greenery that was a background to their table. He knew the kind.

'They're friends of yours?' he asked.

'The woman in red and the man who's smoking have the flat above mine.'

She'd sold some house or other, he heard; a family house, it then became clear. She'd sold it when her mother died and had bought instead the flat she spoke of, more suitable really for a person on her own. Pasmore, the people she had suddenly recognised were called. She didn't know them.

'But they know you, eh?'

He felt quite genial; the diversion passed the time.

'They've seen me,' she said.

'Coming and going, eh?'

'That kind of thing.'

'Coffee? Shall we have coffee?'

He signalled for a waiter. He would go when the wine was finished; usually he went then, slipping off to the Gents, then picking up his coat. Once there had been a complaint to the bureau about that but he'd said the woman had invited him to dinner – Belucci's, it was that time – and had become drunk before the evening finished, forgetting what the arrangement had been.

'I'll hold the fort,' he said, 'if you want to say hullo to your friends.'

She smiled and shook her head. He poured himself more wine. He calculated that there were four more glasses left in the bottle and he could tell she'd had enough. The coffee came and she poured it, still smiling at him in a way he found bewildering. He calculated the amount she'd had to drink: two gin and tonics he'd counted earlier, and now the wine, a good four glasses. 'I wouldn't even know the Pasmores' name,' she was saying, 'except that it's on their bell at the downstairs door.'

He moved the wine bottle in case she reached out for it. The pianist, silent for a while, struck up again, snatches from *West Side Story*.

'It's lovely here,' she murmured, and Jeffrey would have sworn her eyes searched for his. He felt uneasy, his euphoria of a few moments ago slipping away; he hoped there wasn't going to be trouble. In an effort to distract her mood, he said:

'Personally, I shan't be bothering the Bryanston Square Bureau again.'

She didn't appear to hear, although that wasn't surprising in the din that was coming from the piano.

'I don't suppose,' she said, 'you have a cigarette about you?'

Her smile, lavish now, had spread into all her features. She'd ticked *Non-smoker* on the information sheet, she said, but all that didn't really matter any more. He pressed a thumbnail along the edge of the transparent cover of the Silk Cut packet he had bought in the Salisbury and held it out to her across the table.

'I used to once,' she said. 'When smoking was acceptable.'

She took a cigarette and he picked up a little box of matches with *L'Etape* on it. He struck one for her, her fingers touching his. He lit a cigarette for himself.

'How good that is!' She blew out smoke, leaning forward as she spoke, cheeks flushed, threads of smoke drifting in the air. 'I used to love a cigarette.'

She reached a hand out as if to seize one of his, but played instead with the salt-cellar, pushing it about. She was definitely tiddly. With her other hand she held her cigarette in the air, lightly between two fingers, as Bette Davis used to in her heyday.

'It's a pity you sold your car,' he said, again seeking a distraction.

She didn't answer that, but laughed, as if he'd been amusing, as if he'd said something totally different. She was hanging on his words, or so it must have seemed to the people who had recognised her, so intent was her scrutiny of his face. She'll paw me, Jeffrey thought, before the evening's out.

'They're gathering up their things,' she said. 'They're going now.'

He didn't turn around to see, but within a minute or so the people passed quite close. They smiled at her, at Jeffrey too. Mr Pasmore inclined his head; his wife gave a little wave with her fingers. They would gossip about this to the residents of the other flats if they considered it worthwhile to do so: the solitary woman in the flat below theirs had something going with a younger man. No emotion stirred in Jeffrey, neither sympathy nor pity, for he was not given to such feelings. A few drinks and a temptation succumbed to, since temptation wasn't often there: the debris of all that was nothing much when the audience had gone, and it didn't surprise him that it was simply left there, without a comment.

When a waiter came, apologetically to remind them that they were at a table in the no-smoking area, she stubbed her cigarette out. Her features settled into composure; the flush that had crept into her cheeks drained away. A silence gathered while this normality returned and it was she in the end who broke it, as calmly as if nothing untoward had occurred.

'Why did you ask me twice if I possessed a car?'

'I thought I had misunderstood.'

'Why did it matter?'

'Someone with a car would be useful to me in my work. My gear is heavy. I have no transport myself.'

He didn't know why he said that; he never had before. In response her nod was casual, as if only politeness had inspired the question she'd asked. She nodded again when he said, not knowing why he said it either:

'Might our dinner be your treat? I'm afraid I can't pay.'

She reached across the table for the bill the waiter had brought him. In silence she wrote a cheque and asked him how much she should add on.

'Oh, ten per cent or so.'

She took a pound from her purse, which Jeffrey knew was for the hat-check girl.

They walked together to an Underground station. The townscapes were a weekend thing, he said: he photographed cooked food to make a living. Hearing which tins of soups and vegetables his work appeared on, she wondered if he would add that his book of London would never be completed, much less published. He didn't, but she had guessed it anyway.

'Well, I go this way,' he said, when they had bought their tickets and were at the bottom of the escalators.

He'd told her about the photographs he was ashamed of because she didn't matter; without resentment she realised that. And witnessing her excursion into foolishness, he had not mattered either.

'Your toothache?' she enquired, and he said it had gone.

They did not shake hands or remark in any way upon the evening they'd spent together, but when they parted there was a modest surprise: that they'd made use of one another was a dignity compared with what should have been. That feeling was still there while they waited on two different platforms and while their trains arrived and drew away again. It lingered while they were carried through the flickering dark, as intimate as a pleasure shared.

Miami Vice

The whole wife-swapping thing can arrive out of nowhere and before you know it, there it is. On your plate.

We were living in the bungalow outside Birr and it was bleak enough at the best of times. The four walls and a few old fields. I don't know about this stuff where the countryside is supposed to be relaxing you because I nearly went out of my mind. Of course the child was sick half the time. I had fixed up the operation pretty good. I had it lickety-split. People said there was going to be a problem with the chickens but there was no problem with the chickens, none. The problem was a long way from chickens.

They were living inside in the town on a small terrace. It was fairly cheerful. She used to get all done up. She'd be going up to Dublin and coming back in all the gear. He was the man for the jokes and the winks. The wife thought they were the greatest thing since sliced pan but basically they were about the only people we knew. The wife knew her since she was a child and they had been at the afters of the wedding and on a couple of visits for weekends when we were above in Sligo. She was a nice-looking woman and there was plenty of her there. He sold combination socket-wrench sets at the markets. We'd go for a few drinks of a Saturday inside to Dooley's. There'd be music and baskets of cocktail sausages and that sort of thing. It was grand, I suppose. After that, we'd go back to their place on the terrace with a curry. It was always the four of us, the two couples, and nobody else. He started making cracks about it. 'They'll think

we're wife-swapping, John! They'll be saying, who's with who?'
My Mary, God love her, would blush to her ankles. Margaret
thought that it was all great sport.

He was one of these men who always seems to be red in the
face. Breathless-looking, with watery eyes and thick hair combed
back off the skull, always in great form, but kind of like a man
trying to make out he's in great form. He was from the North
originally and he used to wear cheap copies of flashy watches.
Rolexes and that sort of get-up. Contacts coming out his ears, he
said. He liked to make out that he knew loads of criminals.

Maybe six months of the going to Dooley's and the curries and
it was coming up again and again, the same old line. And then
one night he took me aside in the jacks. We were after a few.
'Listen to me,' he whispered, 'what about it? Grown adults, so we
are, and whose business is it only our own? There's no objections
on our side of the fence, John. Margaret thinks you're a very
attractive man and don't be saying you haven't seen her putting
the eyes on you, you rogue! And God forgive me but I'd get up on
that wee Mary as quick as you'd look at me!'

I tried to laugh it off. 'Ah come on now, Frankie, go handy,' I
said. I jabbed him in the arm with my fist and gave an old laugh
out of me. He gave an old laugh back but as he went out of the
jacks he leaned in to my ear and said, 'Sure ye can have an old
talk about it anyway, friend.' Cuffed me on the back of the head
with the big mock Rolex.

To be honest with you the whole thing kind of spoilt the night
on me. He kept throwing out comments. Like about the watch. He
turns around to Mary and says, 'There's links to go on there yet,
it's a bit tight on me.' 'Sure you're a big man,' says Margaret. 'Oh
I am that,' he says, giving Mary a look. She doesn't say much,
only laughs kind of quiet and looks down at her shoes.

I was a happy man to get back to the bungalow. We cried off
the curry side of things. The babysitter drove away home. The

child was asleep at nine o'clock, he told us. Which meant she'd be up at four. Seven years of age and bawling in the middle of the night. Did you ever hear the likes of it? Myself and Mary sat down and got out the gin.

'They're getting worse by the week,' I said.

'They are,' she said. 'But I suppose they're lively at least.'

'You won't believe this,' I said, 'what it is he said to me inside in the toilet.'

'What?'

'Doesn't he start going on about the wife-swapping thing again! In all earnest.'

'Ah he's only pulling your leg.'

'He's serious. He says Margaret would have no bother going with me and he'd go with you. He was full in earnest, Mary.'

I'll never forget what she said next. She said, 'Ah sure, what harm in it?'

I had some week the week after that. Couldn't get it out of my mind, do you know that kind of way? I'd be going around trying to look after chickens and it would be haunting me. Thoughts about Margaret. She was a very handsome woman and you'd be seeing plenty of her. Skirts that went up to there and tops that came down to here. Between myself and yourself and the four walls, she had come into my thoughts many a night. Of course now, Frankie and Mary was a thing I could in no way deal with. The very thought of it made me sick to the pit of my stomach. And I could not get over herself: what harm in it! What harm in it my eye. There were chickens kept waiting for their grub that week. I didn't know whether I was coming or going. I said nothing to your one but by the looks on her you could tell that there was something on the agenda. After a while when you're married there's no great need for things having to be said out loud.

But by Saturday, somehow, I kind of felt that nothing would
come out of anything, that everything would be just ignored or
something and we wouldn't be going to Dooley's. I finished up as
usual about three o'clock and in I come for the few sandwiches.
She's looking at the television and turns around and says, 'What
time are we going to Dooley's? What time will I get washed?'

There was never any formal meeting arrangement or anything
like that. It was the kind of thing where we'd see them inside in
Dooley's around teatime. Half the town would be in there after
the bit of shopping, but the four of us would always land back at
the same table. On this particular Saturday I felt that us showing
up at all was like a signal or something. Of course I had no doubt
themselves would be inside. And sure enough and yes they were,
tearing into the chicken wings and packages of Bacon Fries.
Frankie all kitted up in a purple shirt. Bright purple, now, not a
maroon kind of thing. And jewellery on him like something out of
Miami Vice. Margaret in the shortest skirt yet and a face on her
like she's after eating a bar of lipstick. Chatty as you like, the two
of them. What are ye having, and all the rest of it. And I suppose I
started to relax after a few minutes – maybe he was pulling my leg
all along. The night passed easily enough and there was no
mention of anything, just the usual old talk about football and the
television, and half eleven we're all saying, grand so, curry.

Back on the couch in the front room on the terrace. Curry
boxes everywhere, vodka and beer. Frankie messing with the
stereo and singing along, red in the face. Margaret and Mary
skitting and nudging. Myself getting the bad feeling again. Then
he's up and he's up the stairs and back down the stairs with a
huge pile of sports jackets in all the colours under the sun. 'My
new line,' he says, 'selling like hotdogs so they are.' 'Cakes,' I said,
and I probably sounded kind of bitter. 'Will you do a spot of
modelling for me, Johnny boy?' he says. And I didn't want to
seem like the sour puss. So the next thing the two of us are

parading up and down in front of the stereo in jackets, pushing the sleeves up and play-acting.

'Crockett and Tubbs!' roars Margaret.

And then of course The Eagles is gone on and we're all dancing. And Frankie takes me in his arms, messing, and he says to me, 'What about it, Tubbs?' And Margaret comes in behind me and puts her arms around my stomach and what can I say only she rubs her crotch off my backside. 'What about it?' she says.

The next thing I can remember I'm sitting on the couch with my head shaking back and forwards in my hands and I'm going 'Ah no, no.' And Mary says, 'Ah, John.' And I say, 'Ah Jesus lads, it's wrong.' Margaret sits beside me and rubs my thigh inside and says, 'Still and all, Johnny.'

And this is how it happened that Frankie and Mary walked out of the living room, him looking back over the shoulder and saying, 'Well, we'll see ye in the morning.' Not as much as a peep out of herself. 'Come on, John,' says Margaret, 'we'll head for the bungalow.' 'What about the child?' 'Sure, we won't be waking any child,' she says.

You'd imagine that the wife-swapping kind of thing would take four decisions, but really it only takes three.

'I swear to God to you, John, it wasn't the same,' says Mary. Half eleven the next morning and I was sitting in the kitchen trying to eat a sausage sandwich. And you know there is no bite to eat I like better in the week than the sausage sandwich of a Sunday morning. And I couldn't eat it.

'No, honest to Jesus,' she says, with a big old grin on her face that would shame a scarlet whore, 'it was not the same, it was just all different. I'm telling you, John, all I wanted was to be back at the usual thing. Never again!'

Well, I thought, I either believe her or I go mad. So I tried to believe her and I felt a little better. I took a bite out of the sausage sandwich and squirted another bit of brown sauce in it. I'm a martyr to the brown sauce. Then I decided there was one thing I had to ask straight out.

'Did you come, Mary?'

'Oh, I came about six times!'

Now I did not believe that Mary was a malicious woman. I am not a fool and I know that there are women who have malicious streaks. My mother, now, was a malicious woman, you could even say an evil woman. I'll never forget the night I goes into her room after she's unbeknownst to me after being with O'Donnell and the way she was lying on her stomach and the way she turned around to me and the way she kind of . . . *writhed*, is the only word, like a snake, and the look on her face. Pure hate. But Mary, I felt, was just the sort who says things without thinking about them.

All the same. Six times. I don't want to get deep into this kind of stuff but we might have gone at it twice a week and if she came twice a year it was nothing short of a miracle. There was walls in that bungalow painted more often than Mary came. I don't know how I finished that sausage sandwich but I finished it. Then I went out to the chickens.

The worst of it is when you lose the control of your thoughts. Do you not find? It doesn't happen all that often in life I suppose, but it happens. When you fall in love or when there's a death. You cannot decide for yourself what you're gong to think about, it's all just there, first thing in the morning, last thing at night. And that was about the way of it the week after the night of the wife-swapping. I couldn't get past it.

The worst of it, actually, for me, wasn't connected with the sex angle. The worst of it was that I had crushed two Valium into hot milk and fed it to my crying child to conk her out. It was all Margaret's idea, and they were her tablets to begin with, but what kind of a way is that for a father to be acting? Jesus Christ almighty above on the cross. I'm not ashamed to say that I shed tears myself over doing that with the Valium. Poisoning a small child with drugs because I had a horn on me. All this was worse than the sex angle, but of course there was the sex angle as well.

I'll be totally honest with you, I went close to insane with jealousy. Jealousy is one of the big boys when it comes to the suffering. You hate her and you hate yourself even more. And I felt in my bones that we were only at the start of the thing, I felt in my bones that she'd be sneaking off with Frankie all of the time for her six comes. They'd have to be doing it on the sly because let's face it, there was no way that Margaret was coming next nor near me again. So that deal was off.

Oh it was an absolute disaster. I mean, I suppose we *did*, technically speaking. But it was an out-and-out joke. It had taken some amount of a build-up to get in the gate in the first place. Whether it was nerves or drink or what I don't know. We were there a good two hours before there was any bit of a stir out of the thing. It is an awful curse of a thing when it lets you down like that and only for she started taunting me I don't think we'd have got anywhere at all. But of course as soon as it went in it went and exploded on me. She lay there for the rest of the night yapping nonsense out of her, smoking her cigarettes, saying 'Ah it doesn't matter love, no harm done.' Talking about her tablets. 'That young miss will sleep now sweet as a dream for you, John, you have nothing to worry about there. Those are the English Valium now you know, the old Valium we used to get all along. Until they starts making them below in Clonmel. Clonmel! Oh yeah, they're making them down there now, only they're not the same at all and I'm not the only one saying so. Honest to God, John, you might as well be eating Smarties. But I have an arrangement about the English Valiums with the man in the chemist, the man of the Laffertys. Have you

ever noticed, John, the way every single last one of the Laffertys
has the big teeth?'

I never put down a night like it.

Poultry management is no joke at the best of times. And it's not as
if I have background in it. I come from a town myself. But when
the father-in-law had the seizure there was only Mary and the
business was there and what were we going to do? It wasn't like
we were setting the world on fire above in Sligo. And how much
can there be to do with chickens, I was saying to myself. I got a
queer land when I realised the reality of the situation. And listen,
I'm the last one would ever criticise family but I have to say that
Mary's father, God rest him, was some devil for letting a place go.
If you've ever lived out the country you'll know there is such
thing as a dirty farmer, and I hate to say it but the father-in-law
fit that bill.

It was not a pleasant set-up, really, by any stretch of the
imagination. I mean it was cleaned up a bit and all the rest of it
and there was money gone into it, who are you telling, but it was
not a nice kind of thing on an everyday basis. To make it worth
your while you really have to pack them in. There was a young
lad in town wore one of the long coats was forever buttonholing
me with rants about cruelty. 'What about the quality of life?' he
says, getting himself all worked up. 'What about my quality of
life?' I says. 'Do you think I'm outside in a palace?' But it was true
for him, of course, it's not a way you'd want to see any creature
treated. But what could I do?

The main chickenhouse was bad, now, it was bad. It was dark
only for the ultra-violet and the smell was brutal and they
weren't, you know, the healthiest looking chickens. They cannot
move around in the cages and you have to kind of tie the legs into
them when they grow any bit. And the feed then is not good stuff
at all by any description. But it's funny the way I have mixed

feelings about the chickenhouse. I have mixed feelings because it is the one place my daughter was calm, it is the one place she never cried or screamed. She'd pull at me to take her there and I'd go. She'd sit there on an old pail in her little red coat and it was like she was in a chapel.

To look at now I wouldn't be much. I'm fairly low-sized and I'd have a bit of a gut on me. I wouldn't say I'm ugly but I'm no oil painting. The only thing out of the ordinary is one of my eyes is blue and the other is green. And as things turned out that was the ice-breaker when I met Mary. She was about eighteen years of age and very shy, very gone into herself. I wasn't much older and as it happened I hadn't too much to be saying for myself either. How we ever managed to get a bit of talk going between us at all is one of the divine mysteries. But she mentioned the eyes and that got some bit of a spark flying, I suppose. I wouldn't know anything, now, about love or any of that kind of thing. I wouldn't have the faintest idea about what it might be exactly or whether I've ever actually had a lash of it myself. I know I love my daughter of course but I'm talking about the romance thing, with a woman. There was never anyone much apart from Mary. And we got on grand, you know. We wouldn't be the sort for fire-works. We'd never even really be doing the holding hands or any of that crack, not even when we were younger. I didn't know if I'd miss her if she was away because she had never been away.

And she did go away, of course, not long after the night of the wife-swapping, upped without a word and off to the sister in Hartlepool with a suitcase. She's living with a fella runs a B&B. I was embarrassed more than anything. I couldn't say exactly that I missed her so I cannot say if I ever actually loved her. But you would miss the heat of a woman in the bed at night. She's very thin, Mary, but there was some heat off of her, it used be like she was on fire.

I had enough of chickens, and me and the child are in Sligo again and scraping by one way or the other. I have never seen such a change in a child. She has really come out of herself.

And Frankie and Margaret? We could picture them in Birr, still, ageing slowly in the beautiful light that lingers now on these summer evenings, a little happiness in their faces, even, maybe after a good day at the market in Roscrea and a feed of steak in Shinrone on the way home, and the promise of an evening's drinking opening before them and the interest coming alive in their faces when the doorway is filled with new shadows because after all, you would never know who might walk into Dooley's.

JOHN FLEMING

The Destruction Test

Sputum like chalk, I spit to paint the bare stage boards. Sweat beads are light bulbs in the violent flicker of this white strobe. The audience roar. *Demigod.* I scorch my fist across six electric strings. They reverberate, these telegraph cables stretched taut on my Rickenbacker rack. Tightening to breaking point, they are a barbed wire fence beneath my broken nails. My job? Singer with this hard-core band.

I force the guitar in on itself and play it way past its function as mere musical tool. This guitar becomes a machine again: a wooden body whose slender neck is caught between my thumb and fingers. I play it full throttle. I force noise from its wire and wood and drive it along cables all the way to the mixing desk. Amplified, it bleeds back out of the loudspeakers: guitar-bassdrum chaos. On top sits the thin scab of my voice after its own boxcar voyage through the rust pipes of my throat. Humming and screaming: a hobo. Digging deep into the pit of my larynx, I rifle the history of all the cigars I've ever smoked. This scars the roof of my mouth and makes a vocal picture of sand grains and shards of broken glass. The grit sound result is my singing.

All this introspection when I'm out on stage. It's a type of solitude thing that I share with the crowd. They give me attention and focus – they love me to wild extremes and so afford me the luxury of hating them. One and all: from the little kids, puny and alone, to the pathetic match-dressed couples. Some stand in groups of three or four, drawn together like worshippers, some uniform forming in the tattered disarray of their garb. But it's not about appearance. My show is no fashion show. I specialise in pain. On stage, I deal in damage and hurt. Slouching by the amp rig, I star alongside fear, doubt and betrayal. And we get sold as pop music.

This song we're playing is called *Burnt Candle (Both Ends)*. It has been described as an 'exhaustive dirge' and takes a lot out of me. I don't exactly come fresh to these songs either – this material is brewed in my real life. It's all spill-over from my overwrought world outside – the one I try to share with her. She forces herself into my lyrics. She monopolises my world-view. I dissect our life in what people try to call love songs. I'd argue with their use of the word 'love'. And I don't like the word 'song' either. But I'm not much one for stories and fiction, so these performances and songs are as close as I get to poetry. They give me a living knife-edge and stimulate a direct audience reaction: the kids usually kick back. Through hard work and diligence, I've developed enough drama to put it all over. She makes me sour and sore – she drives me to this. It helps me to sing. I stare in on a raw landscape of nerves and rip out stitches from my old wounds. She tore my heart out years ago. Although my emotions are still real, I now feel her inevitable loss as a logic, as a generalised fear rather than as a knife in my soul. In this song's depth, there feels like no way out. I realise that this is what I have to do. In order to survive, I test myself to destruction.

The songs are grotesque portraits – bad pictures that play up our darkness and layer it with despair. The entire relationship is a divorce, a speeding downward spiral. We both know it just won't work and that's why it does for a little while longer. The fact is that I'm addicted to her. And I know about addictions. She makes me feel like the God I don't believe in. She drags me along East Fifth and in through our spray-paint-scrawled door. She's been dragging me through the months and these months have been growing into years.

Lately, age has become my expert. It arms me – it's now part of my equipment. But it has also started to make me feel outmoded. Vaguely and recently, something in me has broken. I knew my spirit had been wearing down. But it seems that I turned some corner and suddenly it all snapped. In recoil, I see this circus act as all out of sync. A good ten years out. I'm an exhibit from pre-history, a different-decade man fusing the distance and memory of the nineteen-seventies and the nineteen-eighties. She led me to believe I could do this; she even convinced me that I should. She subsidised the adolescence that I have succeeded in carrying this far. But now it's all too late. My civilisation of beer bottles has wound up in a billion battered trash cans. Poking for messages in those bottles, I now can't sleep at night. It's worse than having children. My act is as outdated as my need to make it through this life as part of a heroic couple: I've turned state-witness on Bonnie and Clyde. My new alternative is a return to an old dream: I will be this loveable Bowery bum. I will wear the backside burst out of my real man's suit. I will carry an open forty-ounce bottle of beer in the brown paper bag in which I will soon plant all my kisses.

It still works well together – it's still rough love that she likes. And when I lose it up here on stage, she sees clearly that I am lost in the spaces in myself. In the bend-induced bubbles in my heart. Each is a gulf that bursts as I try to surface from our song. And so I pitch myself against the guitar. It's not an instrument. It's a machine. A machine that can be broken.

I got into this late in the day. Thirty-one. I'd absorbed a zillion bands. In the new thrash pretenders, I saw only pale rehashes. I'd always imagined myself in a band – just one that had never actually formed. But she and the whole East Fifth thing gave me the force to change all that. I needed to have a final stab, some last-ditch attempt before I felt too old. From day one, she pushed me past melody and into this margin of broken noise. Given a type of second adolescence, I realised that it was really my first. I steered clear of the trappings of maturity and felt freedom come out on top. While she slowly knuckled down into a rut, I lived life in group rehearsals. It's not drugs. It's not drink. It's the environment of drugs and drink. A whole world with no horizons and no decisions. For three years, in these backstage-bin changing rooms, I enjoyed the charms of the gang girls. I was amused by the fame in bars and record shops. I felt part of a great inarticulate refusal. I had tired of putting a clear case to peers who don't get it. I've given up on reason and instead use anger. Anyone who uses the word adolescent against you is jealous and truly lost. But these days, after a gig, I just get the hell out straight back home to her and how was her day. I lie there in our domesticated loft and listen to her. It helps me come down slowly from the adrenalin of the gig as it shoots right through me like preservative. I peer through tracing-paper eyelids and wonder when I'll fall from the camera-flash shambles of what we do up there on stage.

They asked me to write a piece for the New York press. I didn't get beyond a vague paragraph about obliterating my guitar through wear and tear. I wrote of testing its timber's metal as I try to break the varnished neck. I wanted to describe how in fact it really resists even as I strain the strings tighter again and painfully lever back the neck. I spoke of strangling notes and of how we administer regular beatings to the drum but, well, one paragraph doesn't make an entire article. But I know we build a net with the noise we weave, a net that catches the little that we have left. We spin tornadoes; we destroy within our fixed radius. Our concerts are a safe zone, a fallout shelter on the very brink of potential, on the very eve of disaster.

So I sleep all day and work all night, filtrating the poison of what I know into songs. I believe melody should be sweet, that melody is the name of a fruit. Music is a pulse and a life-beat, but I make it sound like a punishment and mercy killing. I wade further from the piano-playing singer/songwriter that I adored when I was nine or ten. He sang a refrain about the Northern Lights; its beauty hurt me. It still does. I know I have lost my way. What has happened to make me a butcher, a razor blade, a skid mark on popular music? That's the way it all comes out. I could blame the band – they're a five-dollar barber school quartet of lowlife trailer-park trash, their streaming noses buried deep in dime-store novels and downtown sleaze. But that's the lifestyle around here. It's the stuff this little boy learnt somewhere along the S&M way.

I sat by the Cube monument one night with a beer. Breaking loose from her in the bar, I slid out for a bottle of St Ides and sat in the sea of skateboard punk and pavement graffiti. I stared across at Starbucks and a wine store I hazily mistook for Barnes and Noble. I drank up that August night, creating it as a crystal memory of the passion she gave me. I let the beer backtrack into yeast. Every face became familiar and I knew I was not yet worn out. I saw the hanging-around-on-street-corners-is-power poetics of the city and I turned that poetic into something hard core. It was time for an assault, not a commentary. I'd write songs, not their descriptions. Why window-shop when I could be looting in the smash-and-grab world that had nearly passed me by?

Our songs are four-minute doomed voyages. Just listen to them. They are containers. Forget about words. I'm not a journalist. Jake does swish high-hat drum stuff and drowns my words out – we make language bleed into noise. Our shows have peaks but then doldrums too. Still waters in which the band takes a breather. Fenton nurses his strained shoulder, slipping out of the guitar harness for a welcome pause. Derek rubs his knuckles against his palm, something to do with a recent brawl. I drain a

Perrier bottle and belch there in the stage dark. We just stumble about for these instants in limbo. Jester has been known to go off stage to urinate – he comes back with a newly-lit cigarette. It falls burning from his lips as we launch into the next part of our set.

I'm a soul singer really. That's easy to forget as I lead this team of fallen monkeys through the corridors of each of our dark tunes. I love music: it serves as a sepia catalogue of my past. I feel people like Marvin Gaye and Ian Curtis sitting there on my shoulder as I drag these songs around the stage and dredge up feeling from my sore insides. Dead singers breathe on my neck. We all ultimately sing the same song. Its power *is* emotion. And emotion is violent. That's why I live in fear of emotion. A scuffle erupts at the foot of the stage. I am an antenna for this, I am plugged into what they want. The front row stares back up at me: they are the history of all audiences. As I scrape my plectrum against the strings, I feel pain in the finger caught in our tour-bus door. A black nail for now and always, it's framed like a *Time* magazine cover behind the veneer or my cuticle.

Burnt Candle (Both Ends) builds slowly in a repeating loop of heavy bass. The band doesn't like this one – it strips them of convenient masks. I slap down words, beating the audience black-and-blue to explain family values. I speak of twenty lashes, slowly paced, as the upholstery in an adulterer's back rips wide open. Here comes the hangman for his last public hanging. He is lost in sweet memory of the second and third last one too. We break people, we burst eardrums. We run through the history of torture.

She has destroyed me. She let me push myself to this edge. We are playing a third encore. We're dead on our feet. Forty gigs in thirty days. I can't feel my fingers. I can't hear. I can't see. I can't remember that I love her. Once more, I can't break the guitar. But I cling to it. It's a piece of drifting birchwood. I play a gentle chord and the guitar string breaks. It whips me in the eye. I scream blindly into the microphone.

I can pass this test. She's made me indestructible.

WILLIAM HODDER

The Máistir

The courtyard was small but the freshness of the breeze hinted at
a large sea beyond the hedged fields. The Máistir was grateful for
the swoosh of wind after the confines of the car and the twisting
drive. Forty miles an hour max. Maura's way. And never anything higher than third gear. All the way from Ballynamrock.
Béal Átha na mBroc. The Mouth of the Ford of the Badgers.
Strange, the placenames in Ireland. Very complicated some of
them. A little story behind many, a kind of coded biography of
each little community. Betokened a keen eye, a detailed obser-
vance of the comings and goings once upon a time. Calcified now
of course. Like my joints, thought the Máistir, as he attempted to
ease himself out of the back seat. His life was to all intents and
purposes over once they consigned him to the back seat of his
own car. Resigned all control then. He who always had beautiful
cars. His one folly, Lena used to say. Huh! If only.

Some woman had appeared, dangling a walking aid before her
from an outstretched hand. Zimmer frame, the Yanks called it. He
attempted to shoo her away but nobody took any notice. Maura
was fretting about, Aidan stood to one side trying to think of
something to do with his hands. The Máistir gulped air in order to
clear his head. It only half worked. At best everything only half
worked these days. The strange female was smiling awkwardly,
unnaturally, and yapping on about something or other. She
waved the Zimmer frame like it was some kind of prop and she
the conjuror's assistant. No fear says you, thought the Máistir,

with an arse like that. Maura reached out her hand with that abrupt gracelessness of hers and punched him inadvertently in the shoulder, drawing his attention to his lack of flesh. He felt cold in his bones, though his face, he knew, was as flushed as a toper's. The liver spots on the backs on his increasingly sallow hands gave him the look of a well-looked-after, almost picturesque, leper. He attempted to hawk phlegm. Maura glanced anxiously at Aidan. Aidan coughed, half in embarrassment, half in solidarity. Maura and the other female yapped away at one another, all the while tugging at him, thrusting their determined goodwill under his chin like street vendors. He refrained from snapping. He was in no position to exercise his personality. A man needed to be under his own roof to be a man, or at least to act like one. Else you were beholden. No matter how much you paid. And this place was costing as much as a Swiss chalet but without the quaint cowbells and the year-round snow.

It was a two-storey building and he was lodged on the ground floor, a corner room, en suite and only a toddle – the female's words – only a toddle from the dining room. Eating, to hear her talk, constituted the principal, probably the only pleasurable activity of the day for the residents, outside the basic functions that is. Defecate, micturate, expectorate, salivate and somnulate till you disintegrated seemed to be the routine, the expectation at least. He sighed to himself. He made sure to keep all his sighs private these days. He was old enough to know that the grimmer the expectations, the more precisely were they realised. He had taught classes all his life, been the cynosure of all eyes, met inspectors, ministers, bishops even, as an equal, rebuked recalcitrant parents with a look, merely had to make a noise akin to clearing his throat to call a room to order. Now he adjusted the volume of his sighings for fear of giving offence. He wished that Death, or at least its prospect, could become his friend. Why oh why did he fear it so? His mother had died like a sparrow with just a light leap off the branch of the world into the blue of eternity. It was as if she was a singer who simply let her song fade away, giving over the final notes to a kind of lilt that, without anyone realising the exact moment it happened, became silence.

His room was full of light and had that thief of precious time, a telly. Unnervingly small yet infinitely obtrusive, it perched on a skeletal stand in the corner, demanding homage. In the manner of women Maura fussed for another half an hour, eager to go yet staying well beyond the time necessary for the civilities. Aidan fidgeted and made intermittent observations of relentless banality. Eventually they departed, as did the female who called herself Mary Murtagh. She gave the impression that the alliteration was a deliberate attempt to aid the memories of the senile demented. Afternoon tea, she further announced, happened sometime in the afternoon, he forgot exactly when. He wondered how it would have been if he had had daughters. Sons – and he had three – meant daughters-in-law and they weren't blood. Blood, when all was said and done – and in his case it was – was blood. It was an instinct. It was natural and moral. Blood-in-law, on the other hand, was an obligation and merely a social one at that. He tried to suppress his irritation at Aidan's wordless wave – neither farewell nor salutation, neither condemnation nor tribute – accompanied by the inevitable ducking of the head as if he expected to be douched with water by an unseen prankster, a habit he had had since boyhood. He was always a nelly. We stay in the same grooves all our life, the Máistir supposed, thinking ruefully of himself.

He moved to the window, the inevitable double-glazed uPVC affair, whitely smooth, smoothly white, maintenance-free. He had, he was surprised to note, a view of the sea, of the beach even. A far-off strip of dunes and shingle with a slop of grey beyond indicating the road to America. A road he never took. Never would now. He looked to the sky just as a magpie, magnificent in its formal dinner wear, swooped by as haughty as a Parisian waiter. His life, he felt, was not quite over exactly. Exactly that. Not quite over. Exactly. Not quite. Noises clattered in the corridor outside. The clink of delft. The squeak of swivelling wheels. The whisper of rubber on parquet. Afternoon tea. Already. Suddenly he felt Lena in the room.

'Well, old pal, here I am.' He addressed her without turning around, hands clasped behind his back as if listening to a class chant their multiplication tables. 'Take me as you find me today, day of days.' He almost heard the phantom creak as she perched on the bed, a habit of hers since their early days of marriage, legs crossed at the ankles, swinging loose like a schoolgirl's the first day of the summer hols. He felt as if she glanced quickly about the room with her housewife's eye. He continued to gaze through the window. The magpie had returned to preen himself upon a hawthorn tree, all gnarls and thorns, snowy blossoms long ago shed. Cursed creature.

'Oh, I don't know. It's not so bad. Not as deep as a well nor as wide as a church door, but 'tis enough, 'twill serve. You could have gone farther and fared worse.' He gave an imperceptible nod. Since she died, Lena had developed a tendency to speak in proverbs and quotations, a departure from her sometime norm and suspiciously like his own habits of speech. She had maintained her easy-going sangfroid though, an invaluable gift of the fitfully generous gods which he had never shared. He was, no getting away from it, temperamental. Intemperately temperamental. A wretched, rash, intruding fool? That perhaps was going too far. In fairness to himself.

'Aidan is very fond of you, you know. He was always very shy, especially of you. That's why Maura is good for him. She's got get up and go. A bit like yourself.'

He let out a grunt. Get up and go is right. He never took to Maura. Indeed the three daughters-in-law remained just that, women his sons had inexplicably wived. A widower's spite, perhaps. Seeing other people married, still sharing the same planet, occupying a common space, moving about the same room, breathing side by side through the night in the same bed. Lena was having none of it, of course.

'Mhuise, you're very sorry for yourself today. You see all this as symbolic, of course. You never could just take things for what they are.'

He turned to where he had her sitting, smiling her quiet smile, head angled slightly to one side, grey eyes alive with gentle mockery. He was genuinely surprised to find the bed empty, the covers as smooth as when they were first made up that morning. He smiled in his turn at the empty space. 'It's worse and worse I'm getting, old pal. One day I'll turn around and you'll be standing there in front of me.' He stopped and closed his eyes. The grief had long ago ceased to be a howling beast devouring his heart and pillaging his soul. It had instead transformed into a pack of highly organised rats that never slept but spent all their time hustling about his mind, gnawing away at the little morsels of his sanity that they managed from day to day to forage.

'You're eighty-three, remember. It can't be much longer.'

'You'd be surprised. We're not all fragile little things like you. Eighty-three makes old bones but it's nothing to get excited about these days. Jesus, just a glance around at the inmates here will tell you some of them went to school with God. And *I* have the heart of a steeplechaser.'

After the mere suggestion of a knock the door opened. He had enough time to turn back to the window, his tall bony figure presenting a slightly hunched silhouette in the slanting sunlight.

'This side of the building is so much nicer I always think, facing south-west, I mean. We have the sun all afternoon long. It's something to look forward to in the mornings. Mornings do hang, don't they?'

She was a small wispy old lady with a prominent hooked nose, clad in a floral smock affair as if she had just come from a sketching class. Her eyes were a kind of beady blue and she screwed them up in a disconcerting way from time to time as if she were looking through random gusts of smoke. 'I'm the self-appointed welcoming committee. Nora Mahaffy is my name. Everyone calls me Nonie. Excuse the left hand.' It was light and thin as glass with irregular knobs sprouting about the finger joints. The Máistir felt his own hand grotesquely large as hers lay like a delicate piece of polished bric-à-brac upon his palm. Her right hand remained firmly grasping an aluminium cane which ended in a rubber-tipped three-legged pod. Very steady it looked too.

'Pleased to meet you. I'm . . .'

'Oh, I know who you are. You're the poet, of course. Imagine. I recognised you immediately. From the telly, you know, and that little photo they put on the back covers of your books, though to tell the truth it's just a smudge. Very unflattering. I wonder you stand for it. I said to myself, "My, what's he doing here?" until I realised of course geniuses get old too, don't they?'

'Well, I don't know if I'd go . . .'

'Now now, no false modesty here. We're all family, you know, or at least a close-knit community. Like a village. Yes, that's what we are, a decrepit village. Like Hamelin after the Pied Piper, I suppose. Amazing, it never struck me quite like that before. You're inspiring me already.' She placed a finger momentarily to her lips with the exaggerated solemnity of a child. 'Don't worry, Mr Yeats, I know you're here for some peace and quiet. Your secret is quite safe with me. I'll be off then. You must be exhausted. It's the excitement of your first day. Like going to a new school. It will soon pass. The teachers were horrible creatures in our day, weren't they? Brutes. Especially the women. It's not being married, you know. It withers them up, poor souls.

More to be pitied than despised, no doubt. I never married, or
that's what they all thought. Mother wouldn't have it.' She
paused in the doorway. Its frame made her even smaller, frailer,
more witless. 'A butcher's son. And he was not of our persuasion.
It would never have done. Grandfather had been a Dean, you
know. In a very grand cathedral, somewhere in the Midlands, I
can't recall precisely where. Don't worry. About your secret, you
know. I have lots of them. They keep each other company, you
see. And father said, "You were born a maid, Nonie, and a maid
you'll die." But I said, though I didn't let on, "I was born a maid
and a spinster I'll die." It's not the same thing at all, but father
never did see. He was not a reflective man. Nor indeed was
mother. Come to think of it, she was not a man at all. Yes yes
yes. Not a man at all. Goodbye till next year, then.'

Left alone in the room a fatigue came upon him like a de-
pression, sudden, dank, clinging. He lay down. The bed was hard
and seemed cold. Had it lately done service as a catafalque? Some
old duffer who had eventually fallen off the conveyor belt to be
replaced immediately by himself. Off with the dead, on with the
not quite. His mind blanked as it always did at the thought of
Death. No, that was wrong. Not at Death but at death, his own
personal physical dissolution. Death in the abstract was quite
unremarkable, a curiosity even. The death of others, strangers,
seemed only like the rearrangement of clouds in the faraway
sky, part of the mere variety which made the world such an
intriguing, indeed stimulating, place. But the prospect of oneself
becoming as one with the blankness was simply terrifying. There
was a time in younger, much younger, days when he thought
that a philosophical calm was the reward for the relentless
depredations of age. That, of course, was an arrant nonsense,
part of the arrogant stupidity that makes one's early years so
straightforwardly enjoyable. Age not only sucked the marrow
from your bones, turned your muscles to twine and melted the

brains in your head, it filled the space left behind with a precise personal terror of the end, inevitable and oh so near. Aware of a sharpening chill in the air, he nodded off, surfacing every so often to listen to his snores. When they came to wake him at tea time he felt as heavy and stiff as if he were encased in a rusty suit of armour. Sleep that had once knitted up his ravelled sleeve of care now dropped stitches left and right like a bored hussy too resentful of her mundane chores to discharge them with care.

It was, he discovered, to give Maura her due, a well-appointed establishment. Every *thing* seemed new and, weirdly, every *body* was old, some very old, mere automatons of paper and paste, like giant puppets in a Chinese play. They were, of course, mostly women, elders of their twittering, sharp-eyed, restless tribe, prying, poking and preening in turns just as in their pigtail days. The few men, on the other hand, were waiting, more or less grumpily, more or less mutely, for what could not be long delayed. To be viable they needed the world, and the world had long ago finished with them. They were like relics in a museum waiting for the curator to consign them to packing cases in the basement to make space for other, more challenging, exhibits. The women, the Máistir saw, needed only life to function and that remained to them as long as they could talk and they talked as they breathed, incessantly, automatically, with indiscriminate zeal. He kept to himself as much as possible but the rudimentary civilities were unavoidable at such close quarters. He ended each day feeling as beaten as a tinker's donkey driven home unsold from the fair.

'Christ, old pal,' he grumbled one morning to Lena who stood behind his reflection in the mirror as he shaved, 'I'm like a eunuch in charge of the Sultan's cast-offs in this place.' She was looking solemnly at the back of his neck but he imagined a definite twinkle in her placid pale eyes. Had they always been pale? he wondered. Somehow he thought not.

'A eunuch? That makes a change. You should find it refreshing.'
With that she glided away about her business, humming that
irritating tune of hers. He sulked all day and answered her in
monosyllables that night before abruptly switching off the light.
She departed immediately. She never liked the dark, and even on
their wedding night had insisted on having a night light which
she had specially packed with her trousseau. 'Jesus,' he said at the
time, 'talk about being prepared for every eventuality.'

He lay in the blackness, still tingling with resentment. True
enough he had a weakness for women, this side decrepitude, but
it was an innocent obsession. Look but don't touch was his motto,
and he had lived up to it. He last kissed another woman, how long
ago was it? Fifty-four years last New Year's Eve. A soft, dark block
of a one with short, straight rich-textured hair, a full womanly
face and strong lips, who smoked like a navvy. He'd got engaged
to Lena just the week before and she had gone off to Dree-
moughtar to show off the ring and, in the manner of women,
depress her still-single friends by the very act of reassuring them.
He'd gone to see out the old year at Charlie Higgins' flat off
Dromey Street. Charlie specialised in nurses who in those days
had the name of knowing all about it. One of the other lads
brought a wind-up gramophone and five – he remembered it well
– five Rudy Valee records and highlights from *Showboat*. Charlie
had scraped together a dozen tiny bottles of a strange Tipperary
porter and lashings of lemonade for the girls. The one he ended up
with wasn't a nurse but worked instead in the Public Library,
stacking and stowing books and sending out final warnings. Like
all librarians she had no sense of humour, but she was a good-
hearted girl and soft and warm in his arms as a woman should be.
They kissed and cuddled, sand 'Auld Lang Syne', kissed and
cuddled some more and he walked her home in the frost up
Fallon's Hill, pushing his black jug-eared bike beside him. He
never saw her again and never wanted to, though he could see

she wouldn't have said no. He had long ago forgotten her name but, still and all, she was the last woman not his wife that he kissed; the last, it could be said, of a few.

After a couple of weeks the space within the Home had diminished to zero. Like a raparee he began to take to the hills or, in his case, the slight inclines. The real hills, like real life, were now for ever beyond the dregs of his strength. He turned left along a cracked bóithrín that dawdled off towards the gaunt, grey sea. His legs felt like wet cardboard beneath him. He remembered years ago battering open the sturdy door of the outside toilet with two smacks of the heel of his boot to reveal Tim Murphy and Pa Delahunty huddled inside awaiting retribution. Smoking they confessed to readily enough. Too readily. He'd always had his doubts but, as they say on the cop shows on telly, he could prove nothing.

He looked ahead. The sea was too far away, ducking and weaving between reesky bottoms and wizened clumps of rocks and random bungalows angled peculiarly away from the roadside like cows showing their buttocks to the rain. He had once written poems celebrating landscapes such as this. In both languages. He'd been mildly famous for a time. There had been a vogue for him. But that was long, long ago, in the days when the sergeant actually stopped you at night if you hadn't a lamp on your bike.

The Máistir stood in the middle of the bóithrín trying to recall snatches of his verse, like a shivered tree longing for birds to come and nest once more. Nothing arrived. Not a bird, not a word. When he re-read them the poems now seemed remote, strange. They were still beautiful but it was a passive beauty, lissom, languid, irritatingly forlorn. He missed Lena, but he missed himself more, the self that he had been during the thirty years of his prime, the self he had left behind some two decades ago. That self was still back there somewhere in the empty airless past, still rampaging about full of fire and hope and joy, spitting contempt and anger at the travesty of a world it was forced to live in, penning precious poems to an even more precious posterity and shooting off mighty missives to newspaper nabobs and magazine moguls. For quite a long time he had hoped, indeed he had intended, to make a difference. The World, which had seen off Napoleon and Hitler, didn't even bother walking him to the door; rather it sent its minion, Age, with cracked voice and palsied hand to usher him out into the slush and wind.

The sea was as elusive and as far away as ever. The Máistir turned grumpily back the way he had come. He hated pointless travel, going nowhere, just moving about through a simple aversion to staying put. Ahead of him a clump of children materialised from a shabby cottage and chased each other like a swarm from one side of the bóithrín to the other and back again. He remembered pacing the schoolyard at break, wave upon wave of screeching children breaking upon him day after tedious day, until suddenly by the action of some dark wizard's spell those tiny, trivial, silly days congealed in a moment into forty years and they told him he could pace no more.

'Hello there. You're looking pensive.' The Máistir started. A woman was sitting on the slop-coloured gate, her legs swinging. Looking more closely, he realised it was Lena. This puzzled him. She never came outside with him. And she was different. Her grey hair was auburn now, making vivid the hazel of her laughing eyes.

'You've dyed your hair. It suits you.'

She leaned back alarmingly and gave a brief laugh. She was wearing bright red lipstick, he noticed. He had forgotten that she was a bit of a *femme fatale* in her day. Quite the Lisabeth Scott, though, thank God, not nearly so pouty.

'What'll I do with you? This is my own colour. Auburn. Remember. "Fair Auburn" you used to call me.' He shook his head.

'I was always a bit of an old cod.'

'*All the great writers are.*' He thought of Yeats, Joyce, Tolstoy, Proust, Ovid. She had a point. As usual.

'I'm not a great writer. I'm not any kind of writer any more. I'm just old.'

She grimaced in that way of hers, showing small deep dimples just above the corners of her mouth. '*Don't worry. Your day will come. Our grandchildren will have a fine time on the royalties, believe me.*' To his surprise he did.

She swung herself lightly by her arms and rose up till she perched on her high heels upon the top bar of the gate and looked down on him placidly like a statue in a roadside grotto. He should have been alarmed but he knew she wouldn't fall.

'*C'mon. Up you come.*'

He blinked. 'You must be joking.'

'*Not at all. Just jump, you know the way you did back when you used to train the football team. Remember, you taught Gerry Deane how to field a kick out.*' God, that was a long time ago when the world was only slightly mad. Gerry eventually won an All-Ireland medal with the Minors before drinking himself into a slob.

The Máistir bent his knees and felt the bones crack.

'*C'mon. Jump now.*' She rarely got impatient but he noticed an edge to her voice.

'I can't, Lena. I'll kill myself, for Christ's sake.' He stared at her resentfully. 'Go away, woman, and leave me in peace. You never followed me outside till now. I'll see you back at the Home after tea. This is not the time.'

'*It's the time all right, Domhnall, a chroí. Have I ever steered you wrong? Jump up to me. It's time. Trust me.*'

He bent his knees again and sprang. He suddenly alighted by her side as steady as a hawk and as cocky as a wren. She took his hand in hers in that private way she used to in their courting days when they walked home each Wednesday night from the Céilí in the Legion of Mary Hall.

'*Off we go,*' she said, and with that he found himself rising with her into the air. Glancing down he saw the children, silent now, raggedly converging on the figure of an old man sprawled against the gate, his soft hat tumbling unnoticed down the bóithrín before a sharp wind that had blown up out of nowhere.

Together they continued to rise with a kind of curving gliding motion until he got a full view of the sea, which was not grey at all but a bright blue beneath which shimmered richly purple currents, while along the surface random frissons of saffron glistened like clusters of honeysuckle. The whole scene reminded him of a poem he once wrote about a dream he'd had, and then all at once the words of all the poems he'd ever written and ever read flooded into his memory, darting like exquisite fish among exotic coral, so that he knew his mind was about to explode with the joy of it all.

CORMAC JAMES

Linguini

After three days' absence she comes in the front door at eight-thirty in the a.m. She lets down her hair, kicks off her shoes, with every gesture flourishing her fatigue. I ask where she's been till this hour.

'Time has no mandate,' she says.

This is her answer. This is the latest, this kind of answer. I don't know how we got here, but here we are. Naturally, I am not satisfied with her reply. I feel she has failed in any way to address or even acknowledge the raft of concerns informing my question. Since even silence on her part would have done this to some degree, her reply is to be regarded as an achievement, of sorts. Nevertheless, I see the state she's in and decide this is not the time for an all-out frontal. I decide to bide my time, even though I've been biding it for quite a while now.

I don't ask her if she is seeing somebody. Rather, I suggest she should consider seeing somebody, about her problems. I think this is a fairly shrewd way of introducing that euphemism into our dialogue. Saying this, I imagine her immediate and over-riding concern will be to deny that she has any problems, so failing to register my deft manoeuvre. But instead she declares: 'I am no longer eligible for ill-health.'

I have no idea what she's talking about, but it has the air of being her last word on the subject.

I feel she is avoiding the issue(s), but I don't say this, or not in so many words. I do not want to be combative. From experience,

I've come to the conclusion that she doesn't respond well to direct challenges. I feel that in the event of a direct challenge she would simply 'dig in', like they did in the first World War. I feel that such tactics would be embarrassingly anachronistic. This is a new millennium. I feel that we should have moved beyond such puerile choreographies. I think of men sulking in the trenches, folding their arms – as lately she is inclined to do. Now, I am by no means indifferent to the charms of sullen camaraderie. 'Entrenched', too, seems to me a fine word, deserving of the same quiet admiration as, say, a soundly-built bridge – but only when it does not refer to trenches. Furthermore, in veteran recollection of these current troubles, I would rather not have to encounter the feelings of a humbled child, such as an unequivocal face-off might leave me with. 'There are already far too many humbled children in this individual,' I tell the mirror, poking myself in the chest. Despite my championing of the contemporary, I fell pillaged.

While we are both still recovering from what Marie Carmichael Stopes has termed 'a mature and mutual joy', as if suspecting all that stuff about the 'humbled child,' my wife observes:

'We are perpetually trying to bankrupt the inheritance of our childhood.'

I think she is taking advantage of my weakness for interpretation. She realises, I think, that a mind such as mine could find much sensitivity in this observation of hers. Furthermore, I suspect her of resorting to 'sensitivity' only to cloud the issue, it being general knowledge that she equates this with 'vulnerability', of which it is forbidden ever to accuse her. If I mention the life of the emotions she will say that I and I alone have introduced this into our dialogue, arguing confidently that 'few travellers disembark from the train with no baggage,' or something or that order.

Before I can think of anything appropriate to say, hard on the 'childhood' thing she announces bitterly that there is no toilet paper. There is primal wrath in her eyes as she tells me this. Her concerns seem instinctively to pair themselves off this way, the imminent with the abiding. Trying to relate one thing to another only makes me confused about each individually. The imminent and the abiding. I must choose, she says. One or the other. Although unsure what exactly she means by this, I do not ask. I am afraid that this would confer upon her certain feelings of superiority she does not deserve, but which she would nevertheless draw on to my disadvantage.

I decide that we need – amongst other things – the right time, place and mood to discuss certain matters in a civilised and adult way. Some neutral ground. So, while she is 'in a meeting', I cook dinner, referring to a recipe book every step of the way, leaving nothing to chance. I change my clothes. I light candles. I wait. I tend wicks. A week later, still chained to my post, as it were, I'm woken by the giggle of keys. She staggers into the hall, drunk with sleeplessness. She regards the spread. Lasciviously licking her forefinger and thumb, she pinches out the shivering flames.

'Really, you shouldn't have,' she says, 'brought so much of yourself.'

This may have the outward form of a joke, the same arc and cadence, but I can see damn little humour in it. Idly, she goads the warm wax with her thumbnail, like one keeping her thoughts to herself. I loosen my necktie and decide to eat. It's going to waste anyway, I figure. Why not via me? Probably she'll have something to add to this as well. She does:

'Stop wrestling with that spaghetti as though it were an ethical consideration,' she says, this time without bothering to include even a hint of humour, irony, sarcasm, or any other hint.

What do you say to that? It's linguini, but I hold my tongue. I don't want to be accused of hair-splitting, of introducing super-fluities to a scenario already overburdened with detail. (And besides, the fact of the matter is that I'd made the same mistake as her in the supermarket: somehow, a little air had been trapped inside the packet, it had gone straight onto the *reduced* shelf – they were practically giving it away – and I'd grabbed it without reading the label. *Linguini*, I read when I got home, *freshly made*.) I look from my plate to my wife and back again:

'I'm going to bed,' she says. 'I'm tired,' she explains.

Standing at the window, smoking my after-dinner cigarette, I watch evening's steady silting begin. I watch all night, until dawn settles everything again, as if the waters have been washed clear.

In the morning, she is rested and looks like another woman, considerably improved. I am struck by the way the sunlight strikes her face. She stirs, rolls over and opens her eyes, just a few inches from mine.

'You know, in this light –' I begin to say, but abruptly she raises a hand to stop me, as though I were traffic. She prefers to finish the sentences herself, she says. She says it improves her grammar.

I've had enough. I am inclined, at last, to argue. To have it all out, here and now, with both of us equally awake, both lying here on our bed, side by side, head by head, face to face for once. But we are not equally awake; now I am the one aching for sleep, making me wary of seeing things too much from her perspective.

Later, it is too late. The moment has passed.

Then, in certain actions, she surprises me. Pouring herself a glass of wine, she pours me one too, without asking. From time to time she temporarily relieves me of other desires, unresentfully. Also, in the matter of bills, her will, and so on, she is more than generous, bordering on charitable. I look favourably upon these actions and try to see in them propitious tendencies, as though they 'speak her' more truthfully than any of her actual utterances, which are so far removed from the woman I thought I knew and loved. However, I am of more than one mind on the matter. In weaker moments, I favour the suspicion that these conciliatory gestures of hers are designed to throw me off the scent, as it were, or at least to plant a seed of doubt in my mind. Yes, they are propaganda. If my fears are allowed to lie fallow, it is only that next year's harvest prove all the richer, all the more bumper, so to speak.

Only when she talks to the mirror do I feel I myself am being addressed. 'Congratulations on your beauty,' she cajoles the glass, having left the bathroom door ajar. I do not disagree, but prefer to go on listening in silence, and prevaricate.

I am regularly distracted from my disgruntlements by my admiration for her resilience in the matter of several profound personal griefs. Likewise by my opinion of her carriage, grooming, and so on. I resent these distractions. Somehow they undermine my unhappiness without making me happier, so that I suspect some conjuror's trick, involving dexterity and mirrors. I resolve resolutely to give up these distractions on New Year's Day, like cigarettes.

'Whatever happened to the man who used to come like a well-trimmed lamp into a dark room?' she asks, rhetorically. I would like to devalue rhetoric, but do not know how. I ask my friends but they think it's a trick question, and refuse to be tricked. I tell them I am sincere. Sincerity is the new irony, they reply definitively. I try to think of something that cannot be construed as other than sincere, but in the meantime keep my mouth shut, counselling myself with the fact that discretion, valour, et cetera.

Or: 'I was so naive,' she says. I feel we may be getting somewhere, at last. 'Once upon a time, whenever you spoke I was seized with fear –' Yes? '– the fear that you were going to ask me to join a religious cult.' My hopes have proved unfounded. 'I am no longer afraid,' she tells me, and I believe her.

'The art of complaining is dead,' she announces slap bang in the middle of truceful banalities. At the end of my tether, or quite near the end of it, I ask her bluntly what this is apropos of. She refers me to a chapter headed *Common Errors In The Use Of Prepositions*. I feel crudely outwitted. Those who have many problems, she says – as if in saying so she is automatically excluded from consideration – cannot deal with them all simultaneously. It is a question of prioritising, apparently. First things first. Begin with the basics, she impugns. Certainly, I *feel* impugned. In certain areas, one must learn to concede to those with superior knowledge, she harangues. I feel harangued, though simultaneously grateful she's not operating at full mental and intellectual capacity, because of lack of sleep. I dread to think what a drubbing I'd get were she firing on all cylinders. At this point, it occurs to me that my vocabulary had grown since coming to know her in an intimate way. Should I be grateful to her for this? Would she deserve the benefits of such gratitude? I'm unnerved by the notion that, literally or no, my wife's bedfellow is not the man she married.

In the mass media, a person states that he really needs to talk to someone, although he does not name names. Maybe this is what I am feeling. Certainly, I want to know the unnamed name. Maybe this thing is bigger than me. Maybe it is a general malaise. As if on cue, the telephone rings. It is my mother's ring, which I recognise immediately, with dread.

'Next time you come over,' she says, 'don't forget to let us know beforehand whether or not you're married. I'll always be glad to meet the wife.'

There's a malice in her words I can't quite put my finger on. I do know, however, that despite all our problems I don't like this way of referring to my wife as 'the wife'. Not alone does she occupy a particular – as opposed to generic – role, but (in my opinion) she occupies that role in a very particular way. I cross my mother off the list of unnamed names. I begin compiling two lists, in my spare moments. One list is of those persons who should be crossed off the list of unnamed names, when eventually that list is compiled. The other is of those persons who should be added to or allowed to remain on that list, when eventually it comes into being. I hold that event – the simultaneous generation of these two lists, mutually begotten and sustained – before me as a horizon, sometimes near, sometimes far, but a horizon towards which I am ceaselessly and tirelessly working, in my spare moments.

The convention is only two days away. I hear her practising her big speech again, before the mirror.

'My dear contemporaries, et cetera,' she says. 'You feel, perhaps, that you have come without an invitation, or that the invitation was general. Well, I am here today to tell you –'

Unusually, it's the opening more than the ending she's dissatisfied with. I am no help, she says, which strictly speaking is true. I know that if I said anything she would frown and sigh and tell me that I am no help, no help whatsoever, so I have said nothing. I have learned to keep out of these things. I am still learning. In a bar (I allow myself the occasional drink nowadays) I heard someone say: 'You must let them make their own mistakes,' and felt this was the type of conversation I should be involved in. For a long time I studied the speaker, in whom I thought I had recognised something of myself, but he looked like any other stranger: strange. Eventually he returned my stare, looking equally baffled by a lack of recognition.

In what, retrospectively, I consider to be one of her lighter moments, she confronts me in the elevator, where there is little chance for deferral or deflection.

'There was a time,' she says, 'when you were more exotic than instant noodles.'

I accuse her of sarcasm, amongst other things. She roundly denies the charge of sarcasm, with a watertight alibi: sarcasm is one of the last chapters of the intermediary level, and she is not yet even finished basic. I suspect her of studying in secret, but won't hold my breath for a confession; she has too much to gain from her own achievements, even at levels she's not yet meant to have superseded.

Not to be outdone, however, I am preparing several speeches of my own. My favourites are those which are 'tinged' in some way – with pessimism, Hellenism, or other tinges. I want the speeches to have a dark secret, which will cause speculation as to how much I might be leaving unsaid. In the hope of bringing us closer together, here and there I leave a gap which she herself may be tempted to fill, like a lone parking space.

'It was not I laid the axe to the pine,' I speech, 'My hand was not waiting – merely empty and open. How was I to know this was where the oar would fall?'

I am quietly impressed and hopeful. I bide my time. Delivery and context are crucial.

Six months later, she walks in the front door, completely unannounced and unapologetic. It is the small hours of the night, but she shows no signs of weariness. On this occasion she is given to fevered exclamations, like a woman possessed. She has been to a jazz concert – a 'gig' – at an intimate venue, and feels obliged to enthuse.

'Such incident precision!' she enthuses.

She is zealous. She describes her condition as 'wired'. Since I last saw my wife, her vocabulary seems to have expanded in several unexpected directions. Imagining the circumstances of these expansions disconcerts me. Later still, she offers yet another description of the performance:

'Like a series of perfect accidents!'

Bizarrely, the insufficiency of her own descriptions only seems to excite her further. But I do not object. This is something I could get used to. In fact, in a roundabout way, I appreciate her enthusiasm, it being something I've not observed in her in some time. If I cannot share her joy, I nonetheless nurture and indulge it as best I can. I am hopeful that this new-found *jouissance* might spill over into other areas of her life, closer to my own concerns and needs. That said, I don't think I should force anything. I am willing to let this process mature at its own natural pace, and become general, perhaps. Or at least *more* general. Perhaps.

Such a new dawn, I feel, might not be the best time for admonitory speeches. Besides, I say to myself, I have rehearsed my speeches well and often, and can give as able a rendition in any situation. I bide my time. Ripeness is all, I counsel myself. I feel ripe, as I have felt for some time now, and as I expect to feel for some time to come. All I have to do is wait. The night she first left, I wanted to go out into the city, to search for her, but my mother told me to stay where I was. 'She'll come back,' Mother assured me. 'In her own good time.' And Mother was right. Patience.

In the meantime, again and again, my mind casts back to the first time ever we came face to face, when she repeated for me something her father once said, on hearing she was 'seeing' an older man, a divorced man. I don't remember the phrase exactly, but it involved the father imagining his daughter being 'left on the shelf'. (The term 'soiled goods' or 'spoiled goods' was also used, I seem to recall.) Now, could any sane man fear his daughter would *literally* end up on a shelf? No. Could he confuse her with something she is not and never could be – such as a can of tomatoes? No. No, what's unsettling is the staunchness of this fact, before any gloss I might hope to put on it: that the man who had generated and educated this girl, guided her through sorrows and perils, worried at her vagaries and relished her progress, familiar as any husband – that this man could *nonetheless* think of her in such terms! At the altar of God, what rotten hull did he think he was handing over to me? Horrible! Horrible!

She repeated for me what her father had said, and added nothing more. No explanation as to why she chose to share this anecdote with me, a total stranger to her at the time; but none was necessary, it seemed. No, looking at her then, I seemed to hear echo between us a cry too simple, too flagrant to merit a voice: 'Here I am! Here I am! I'm waiting! I'm waiting!'

That feels like a long time ago now. Again and again, I think of that echo I imagined filling the space between us, the first time ever we came face to face. Did I only imagine it? All I can say is that lately – though I know not what – I'm beginning to suspect her silence meant something else, something else entirely.

WILLIAM WALL

The Bestiary

It strikes him then that there are portents, that anything may be a sign – objects and their arrangements, their disposition in regard to other things, the colour, the texture – that the world is a wilderness of significance.

For an instant he is uncertain of his place in the lecture, the words on the paper dissolving, their edges bleeding into each other. He hears the pens scrabbling, the shuffling of feet, the whispering. His head is saturated with sounds and there is no place for the word. He sets his finger down and follows the finger to the paper and finds that the letters are disjointed, blurring, more like watery hieroglyphs or random etchings on a rough plate.

Which is it? he wonders. Hieroglyphs or random marks? Is there a message?

He is assailed by the knowledge of his own inadequacy, his unpreparedness, his lack of skill in the kind of ciphering required to understand these phenomena. He listens carefully and hears a tiny scrabbling sound, and behind that, a distant susurration akin to water on a pebbly shore or voices whispering in a nearby room. Panic grips him again, but only for a moment. This time a name reaches out to him from the page. *Tradescant*. It has a comforting bourgeois sound, an ordinariness that reassures him. John Tradescant extends his hand through four hundred years to rescue him from confusion. Something concrete. Like his own name: Tom Ryan meet John Tradescant.

He has a fleeting picture of the elder Tradescant, the Royal Gardener, tramping heavily through his park of curiosities circa 1650, plants brought from distant lands (so many suffixed *tradescantia*), the wonder of all England.

After all, he thinks, I am a little overwrought, no more. I need a holiday. Perhaps I need glasses. The thought comes to him that he may be lonely, hence the phenomenon of a middle-aged lecturer who seeks out the comforting presences of the long-dead, a bachelor in a third-class university plundering history for companionship. But on the other hand, what else would a scholar be?

He looks up now, fills the lacuna with a dissembling cough, and raises his voice to tell them that their research must reach as far as the Tradescants, *père et fils*, 'the first rumblings of the bizarre as a public obsession, not just the preserve of scientists and royal collectors'. The phrasing pleases him. This is the controversial subject of one of his first scholarly articles, snarled over by experts in the field at the time, his own pet theory.

He is in full flight then, silencing the scrabbling, the voices. The disturbing awareness of meaning in everything that has elated and depressed him in recent weeks fades away. He is never so happy as at a lecture, he tells himself, ignoring the cold sweat that is starting at his armpits. He pulls the comforting name out again. Tradescant. And the anxiety is stilled.

'They were not just botanists who gave their names to a number of useful garden plants, but also, I contend, the originators in English literature to the present day, of our fascination with the bizarre. If I tell you that their public collection of curiosities included, and I quote,' he shuffles his papers dramatically, not needing to, but enjoying the tiny hiatus, sensing the poised pens and eager eyes, ' "two feathers of the Phoenix tayle and a natural dragon above two inches long." That's from the catalogue of 1656. You get the significance?'

When it came out his article had caused a satisfying controversy, but in the end the scholarly consensus was simple: he was wrong. They had no doubt about it and proceeded to ignore the thesis in all future work. Not for him the scholar's modest pleasure of seeing his name quoted in footnotes. It was a kind of oblivion. Nothing he had written since had raised so many hackles or, for that matter, come close to reaching the footnote threshold.

He stares up at the stacked theatre, the benches rising tier upon tier, nuns in the front, louts at the back, the great mass of those who could not do and would teach instead in between. From where he stands their heads are on an elevated plane so that although they bend assiduously to their work he is looking directly into their faces. Mostly girls. One or two beauties as always. What brought them to a module on Beasts & Horrors as Motifs in English Literature (10 lectures)?

'I'm going to leave it there for today because, as you know, there is a reception in the Staff Common Room where an unconscionable quantity of free wine is available for those who appreciate such things.'

He stops again. He does not intend to go to the reception but he likes them to think of him as a Rabelaisian reveller. In fact, he will hurry home to his study. He shivers at the thought: the tiny echoing room, the blank paper, the gloomy books, the noise. He wonders if perhaps he has rats hiding somewhere in the cavities or under the floorboards, their scrabbling echoing through his conscious thoughts even when he is away from home. He shakes his head briefly to banish them and sees one or two students nodding to each other. They watch every move I make, he thinks.

I have begun to develop tics.

I must stop shaking my head.

'As regards free drink, students need not apply.'

There is a ripple of laughter. They like his wit.

'Let me just recommend something hot off the presses and not available in the library. Marina Warner's new book *It's No Go The Bogeyman*. I suggest sleeping with a rich medical student who'll buy it in hardback for you as a gift.'

The joke goes down well. Chuckles as the class breaks up, the louts making for the door, heavy-booted, talking loudly about football; nuns gathering paraphernalia; people moving up and down the theatre steps. The fleeting impression of a vast companionability.

He sees an angular girl in black leggings, black padded plastic jacket, hair cut tight. She swings down through the moving crowd, a counter-flow, and the crowd separates to let her through. She is looking directly at him.

'Excuse me,' she says while still two steps up from the floor. 'About this Tradescant guy?'

He smiles and nods. She takes the last two steps quickly and suddenly is standing in front of him, legs splayed, one hand in the pocket of her jacket, one clenched in a tight little fist at her side. He sees no evidence of an A4 pad.

'What I want to find out is, is this guy Tradescant worth chasing up? I mean does he exist even?'

'Oh yes,' he says. 'John Tradescant exists all right. Existed, I should say. In fact there were two of him, father and son. In fact, his collection was the foundation of the Ashmolean Museum in Oxford.'

'Only I don't want to go after some fucking gardener, do I?'

He is taken aback by her language and answers severely, professorially: 'But we are not interested in the people here, we're after the roots of the metaphor.'

'Yeah, right,' she says. Standard modern expression of disbelief. 'Only I chased up Lyly that you mentioned last week. What a boring fucking book. *Euphues*. I mean we're talking about the Barbara Cartland of the fucking sixteenth century here.'

'But very influential,' he parries. The lecture theatre is empty and his voice has a curious hollow reverberation. 'I quote: "That beautie in Court which could not parley Euphuism, was as little regarded as she which now there speakes not French." Charles Blount.'

'Yeah, right. Whoever he is.'

She is bored.

'Look, I have this reception I mentioned.'

'Yeah, right. The free wine.'

'Exactly. The free wine.'

'Only this is the third lecture' she says. 'And you're still in the fucking dark ages.'

He wants to say that it's not the fucking dark ages, and that the whole point of his course is to establish the roots of literary horror in its historical context and that she would have to wait another five lectures before he came within an ass's roar of the twentieth century. But he is aware of his own blind spot. I'm comfortable enough in the past, he thinks. It's the present that worries me.

'Well stick around,' he tells her. 'If you can take another two or three hundred years of gardeners. And let me remind you, apropos the references and so on, that the failure rate in my class is just over thirty per cent per annum.'

Her look is withering, an incipient snarl rucking the upper lip. She sighs and swings away from him. He watches her go up the steps. One of those aggressive students that he got sometimes, cross-overs from some other discipline, commerce or psychology, where they had an unshakeable conviction that a few units of Eng Lit would teach their students to write better reports. Horror always drew them. She wouldn't last long. She was probably attracted to his course because she thought he would cover Stephen King. Her patience would wear out.

She turns at the top, one hand holding the swing-door. She

calls down to him as he gathers up his papers and opens the mouth of his leather case.

'I'll check it out,' she says. 'I'm probably the only one in the place who follows up your fucking references.'

And she is gone.

He detects a faint shimmer where she had been, like a ripple in space, an after-image of the door and her body, their angular shapes thrown into some hieratic relationship.

Who is she?

The air is suddenly charged with sex: rank and saucy, potent, confounding him.

Three nights he dreams of her. When he wakes after the first night there are some lines of poetry in his head: 'Sure thou wast born a whore even from the womb of some rank bawd, unsavoury as a tomb, who, carted from all parishes, did sell forbidden fruits in the highway to hell.'

Thomas Carew, he thinks. What put that there?

He remembers his dream. She is on her knees, her leggings dragged down around her thighs. He ruts into her, sweating, and as he ruts she talks, foulness streaming from her.

The smell.

But what is the end of the poem? He finds it in his study, a forgotten anthology: *Minor Poets of the Seventeenth Century*. 'And let no man ever bemoan thy case that once did know thee in the state of grace.'

He holds the book close to his face and scrutinises it. By now he knows how it works. There is always some way to reach him. It is up to him to be alert. The dream, the poem, the book, are indices. He must bend all his thought to elucidate them. He holds the book to the light of the window. There are marks in the margin, almost-letters, half-characters. The smell too is important. Dry paper? A suggestion of glue?

An hour passes in the study, the background filling with the sound of small things in the woodwork, distant insinuating voices. When he puts the book down to rub his palms over tired eyes he takes the time to listen and can distinguish occasional words: strumpet, Ishmaelite, infanticide, grace. Isolated cells of innuendo. The connective tissue between them is lost, burned off in a fever of listening and reading. When he puts the book away the noise is suffocating. He shakes his head but there is no diminution. He rushes into his clothes, catches up his coat and bag and goes, slamming the door behind him.

The crash restores silence.

It is the quiet time, mid-hour, in the student restaurant. Tom queues patiently while a pair of girls argue with the person at the coffee urn about getting decaff. In the end the woman shrugs her shoulders and says 'It's what they gives me, girl, I don't buy it meself.' The two girls glare at each other and ask for glasses of water. He notices that they have oozing burgers on their trays, a pile of flaccid chips, sachets of ketchup, paper packets of salt and a pool of urine-coloured vinegar.

He takes his tray (tea and a Danish pastry) to the furthest table, his briefcase jammed under one arm. He lowers the tray carefully and drops the briefcase. It falls with a dead sound, papers rather than books. There was a time when he always carried a book with him, when he was still alive with the discovery of each new joy, when he was still publishing regularly – poetry and scholarly articles. A time when he would take two or three days in Dublin, browsing the Folklore Commission, the Chester Beatty, lunch with someone else in the field from Trinity or UCD. Today he takes his lecture notes out and arranges them on the table in front of him as a blind, hoping to appear busy. He clips the top off his pen and puts it beside them.

An alibi, he thinks. I need an alibi for being here. The truth is

these papers represent idleness, not work, intellectual *rigor mortis*.
I have ceased to think. Someone said it about Ronald Reagan –
that the lights were on but there was no one home.

He cuts the Danish in four, the thought of Reagan reminding
him that Henry Kissinger always had a half-dozen for breakfast,
and is about to pick up the first piece when he sees her come in.
She saunters uncertainly to the counter and buys a coffee. He
specifically hears her ask for instant, significantly cheaper than
the black oil that is kept burbling on the Cona. She fills the cup
with milk and looks around.

He lowers his head, picks up the pen and begins to scrutinise
the top sheet.

Let her not fasten on me, he thinks. I could do without this.

Then she is standing in front of him. She does not introduce
herself.

'I checked it out,' she says. 'Your fucking gardener reference.
It's under Botany.'

Wearily he looks at her. 'I did say.'

'You're a jerk-off,' she says. She is angry and he notices that
anger makes her interesting. There is a small red spot on her
cheek and that curl of her lips that he noticed in the lecture
theatre is half-snarl, half-smile.

'Look miss,' he says. 'Why don't you sit down and we'll talk
this over. I think you're missing the point.'

'What is the fucking point? That's what I want to know. When
I started here I was expecting that at least someone would have a
fucking brain. Instead of that I get fucking old farts everywhere.
Boring bastards with Anglo-Saxon and Modernism and all that
stupid shit. I mean, what do they think it's actually about?'

'What?'

'Fucking literature, that's what. It's about something, isn't it?'

'You've lost me.' He is uncomfortably aware that she is looking
down on him, that when he looks straight ahead he is facing her

groin where the elastic leggings provide him with a view of what appears to be a cleft low down in her *mons pubis*, a suggestion of another smile altogether less angry and more dangerous. The state of grace. Sweat is suddenly pungent at his armpits, between his thighs.

'Right,' she says. She puts her coffee mug down on the edge of page three of the notes, a tiny splash spreading sepia over the blue ink, a blue fizz growing on each letter. She pulls off her plastic jacket and reveals a black top ornamented with heraldic flowers and transparent in places, a black bra clearly visible under it all.

She must be so cold. How do women walk around in November with so little on? Skirts? Blouses as thin as crêpe paper, thinner sometimes. I am always cold. They metabolise more quickly, bodies burning up with fierce energy, while I am sluggish, clogged with sloth, torpid.

'Want to know why I came to college?'

He shrugs. He knows. He has heard it before five hundred times.

'You're probably thinking, working class, poor family background, wants to get ahead. Right? Dead wrong. Dead wrong about one thing. I don't give a shit about getting ahead.'

She is or is not working class? Which? No need to ask. Look at her. And the word *fuck* should be a give-away but is not these days.

'The reason I came here is because I was stupid enough to think that people who had brains actually used them. I expected people would talk about real things. Instead of that it's all second-hand. It's everybody else's idea of what happens, that's what the whole thing is about. It's all fucking *criticism*.'

The contempt is palpable.

'You should transfer to Philosophy,' he says wryly, 'they have a much better handle on reality.'

She stares at him. He takes a quick nervous gulp of tea and feels the scald on the back of his tongue and throat. A bite of pastry fails to assuage the hurt.

'Just tell me one thing interesting,' she says. 'One thing interesting that's going to come up in the course. Or else I'm gone.'

'Look miss, you mightn't believe it but I don't give a shit whether you're in my course or not. My salary isn't based on having you in it.'

He can hardly believe that he has risen far enough from his torpor to be angry. He hears his own voice at a distance and is able to marvel at it, a phenomenon, a thing in itself.

'That's it so. I knew it all along.'

'What now?'

'You're just another boring fart.'

Taken aback, he smiles first.

'You don't put a tooth in it.'

'It's so fucking . . . British. Put a tooth in it. Law de daw.'

'You're just trying to get up my nose.'

'Just one thing? One little teenshy weenshy thing?' She flashes a smile at him and leans forward so that he can smell her breath and it smells of apples and coffee, a heady mixture of open air and Nescafé, sweet and sour. The tilt accentuates her breasts which are the only opulent part of her, full and generous, no angles. The whole thing is suddenly, unbearably erotic.

'Just tell me one thing.'

'OK,' he says. 'One thing.' He inhales slowly, filling up with her, his head spinning on the mixture.

One thing, he thinks. I need one thing interesting.

Out of the corner of his eyes he catches a glimpse of something brown, furtive, in the scrawny plants outside the window. A small bird, or a rat scavenging. The movement unnerves him.

'The next lecture is on *The Bestiary*,' he says. '*The Physiologus*. Ever heard of it?'

He wipes a line across his forehead with the back of his hand. When he looks at it the skin is dry. Where has the sweat gone?

He tells her about the ancient *Physiologus* – bawdy, didactic, crude in the extreme. He outlines the manuscript's history: its putative beginnings in Alexandria, transformation at the hands of early Christian scholars, translations into Ethiopian, Syriac, Arabic and Latin. The synod of Gelasius in 496 which banned the text. She listens and drinks her coffee. At first she is remote, evaluating his performance from that distance which she had set up herself. But she is drawn in. The crowds come between lectures and go out again. The staff behind the counter changes. Almost an hour passes before she interrupts. By then she is leaning forward again. Their heads are close. Her eyes are bright, her mouth hangs open a little.

'So,' she says at last, 'what's in it? Why did Gelasius ban it?'

He notices that she gets the name right. Sharp.

'That's the whole point of the lecture,' he says. 'You have to go to find out.'

'No it isn't,' she tells him. 'The point of the lecture is a fucking reference. It's a jerk-off. It's you giving us something to do and justifying the department hanging onto you. Or have you got tenure?'

He is surprised by the question, the terms of the question.

'I'm permanent.'

'You never said a truer word,' she said. 'OK, I'll look it up.'

She gets up to go.

'No, hang on a sec,' he says. 'Sit down. I'll save you the trouble of coming to the lecture.'

She sits down suspiciously.

He tells her the bestiary story of how the female elephant seduces her mate by offering him the mandrake root. He explains the moral drawn by the early Christians, that the Adam and Eve myth is refracted throughout the natural world, that the female is always dangerous.

'Do not become ensnared by carnal pleasure, or you may be slain by the devil. Wine and women easily seduce the man of God. That's the meaning of the tale. But it goes back further than the meaning you see. The elephant and the mandrake root are primeval sex. They are the open carnal nature that the Church must suppress.'

'Yeah, right,' she says. But he knows from the tone that it is not incredulity. Carnality is in the air between them, a tangible presence. He shivers at the recognition.

'Or the hyena which was said to have a stone in its eye which allows a man to see into the future if he keeps it under his tongue.'

She rocks back on her seat and stares at him. 'I'm sorry,' she says. 'I was really pissed off that time earlier. I went too far.'

He shrugs. 'It's OK. I deserve it.'

She smiles and puts a hand down on his where it holds the biro horizontally over the page. She says nothing. Her nails are painted green. The hand rests there no more than a second but he has time to feel its bones, its sinews, the insistence of its pulse. He senses that metabolism that burns them up, women, consuming them in fractious haste. He thinks when she takes it away its imprint will be there, the life-line and love-line of her palm etched in negative on the back of his hand, but when she does there is nothing left. He looks at the back of his hand and it is the same.

'Gotta run,' she says, and almost immediately she is up and headed towards the door. He shouts goodbye and she nods her head. She may have been saying hello to someone on the way down, he is not sure.

She didn't come to the next lecture, and although I laid my wares out much as I had done for her that day in the restaurant, no other student seemed so taken by *The Physiologus*. I checked afterwards and the three texts I recommended were not disturbed in their dusty stack. Two weeks later she was there again, sitting halfway up the steps, a red jacket and blue shoes. I could see the shoes because she sat in an aisle seat, twisted sideways, one foot cocked out over the steps.

I was talking about animals with reference to the bestiaries and the collection and advertisement of freaks, and she had a notepad and a biro and occasionally put in furious bursts of writing. In between she chewed the pen-top with a look of intense concentration.

'The composers of bestiaries projected their own obsessions onto the animals they described,' I was saying. 'As a consequence, the bestiary is a good indicator of what was considered taboo, or simply bad form. The underlying agenda of the Holy Mother Church is everywhere of course, especially the sexual one. Sex and dirt. Sex and shit.'

That was for the nuns. And for her.

I had noted this trend in my lecturing – the crudity, the urge to shock, delight in offending the prurient. Lecture after lecture nowadays, no matter how I swore to be clean-mouthed.

I had time to wonder how my course had taken this scatological turn. I saw the pile of manila folders that constituted my notes for the same course, delivered last year and completely different, sanitary and safe, stacked untouched on the floor beside my desk. The new ones, piled high, scribbled all over, tumbling with ideas. Not for the first time the thought struck me that I was on the verge of the greatest discovery of my life, that the prodding and shocking was all part of an inexorable progress towards an overwhelming truth. The existence of this truth, a shimmering form on the edge of consciousness, drove me on, at the same time a justification for the grossness and the imagined object of it.

So I told them about the weasel which was held to be a

disgusting animal as a consequence of the female's habit of receiving sperm into her mouth. How she delivered her young through her ear.

How it was forbidden to eat weasels.

How the viper inserted his head into the mouth of the female and ejaculated down her throat. In her carnal ecstasy the female bit off the head of her mate.

How it was forbidden to eat vipers lest the practice become current among Christians.

How hyenas were reviled because they changed sex annually, clearly unacceptable in the Judaeo-Christian tradition, and imitated the sound of vomiting in order to attract Good Samaritans whom they ate. Given the injunction to visit the sick, I suggested, churchmen could not be expected to approve of such practices.

There was more in that vein, delivered to a tittering audience sprinkled with irate nuns. I finished on excrement and urine and a flourish of Sir Thomas Browne on toads.

'Finally, as a coda to all of this, let me quote Browne, see last week's lecture for the reference, on the question of whether, as he so succinctly put it, "a Toad properly pisseth, that is distinctly and separately voideth the serious excretions."'

I took a deep breath, checked that I did in fact have the quotation written out, and was about to deliver Sir Thomas's admirably crude estimate of the answer when I heard someone say, 'Excuse me.'

I looked up and she was half-propped on her seat, elevated but not standing, one hand in the air. Her fingernails were red.

'A question, no less?' I said weakly. 'Just what I've been waiting for.'

'What I was wondering is, is this stuff about piss and shit meant to shock us, or is there going to be a question on it or something?'

I saw the nuns nodding their heads to each other. Everybody

else tittered. I felt my bowels freeze suddenly, something down there in spasm, the urgent need to go to the gents.

'Both,' I said, and smiled. I was hoping the smile was disarming.

'OK,' she said. 'Well I'm not shocked so it's a fail on that point. I checked up on the Tradescants and nearly everything in their collection was authentic, botanical stuff. You just threw that in because they were gardeners by profession and you thought it would piss us off, which I find objectionable. Most of the stuff you're talking about now is covered in a book called *Beasts and Bawdy*, by Ann Clark, published by Dent. I have the reference and it's in the library. So, what's the point?'

'Actually, that is the point.'

I was playing for time. I was lost. And I was listening to a tiny sound coming from behind me, behind the wooden panelling at my back. They have rats here too, I thought. The country is full of them.

'What, actually?'

'That you checked the reference.'

'That,' she said, 'is fatuous in the extreme. If I wanted to learn about a fucking library I'd have got a job in one.'

The theatre erupted. Louts hooted, nuns chuckled, the can-dos and the teachers haw-hawed and elbowed each other. I was defeated.

When the noise died down I waved my hands and smiled, aware that there was something desperate in my smile, and said, 'All right ladies and gentlemen, after that devastating critique I'll call it a day. Next week we'll be coming up to date a little. We'll deal with the unicorn and the maiden and the self-destructive habits of beavers who castrate themselves when they are trapped by hunters.'

The theatre emptied quickly and by the time I had shuffled my notes into my briefcase she was gone.

I don't know what happened to the rest of the afternoon, but at five-thirty I found myself in the College bookshop. I was buying her a copy of Ted Hughes' *Crow*. And I was crying.

He has conceived the notion that she is hiding somewhere on the campus and so he rushes blindly from student bar to common room. He trawls the hidey-holes: the shaded seats of the President's Garden; the pond; the social areas; the library. She is not there. He waits for the turn of the hour and watches people spilling from lectures. It comes into his head that she told him she was doing classical studies and so he follows students to a room where a patrician foreigner lectures on Stoicism and Seneca. He does not recognise the man.

He leaves the lecture and comes out into the cold evening air. He is aware of panic growing like an animal in his gut. How could she do it to him? He remembers how he laid out the story of *The Physiologus* for her, trying to make it interesting, trying to make her feel she was not wasting her time. It was an invitation: this is my world. She could have looked at it and understood because everything was there: the scholarship, the loneliness, desire. She had responded by humiliating him.

It is a sharp November night, full of woodsmoke and crystal stars. He sits on the bench opposite the Student Common Room and tries to calm himself. After a time he notices that he is shivering.

He remembers her thin face peaking at a sharp nose, her thinness in the elastic clothing, the energy emanating from the touch of her hand.

By an effort of will he imagines her sitting in the second chair in his study, the one he reserved years ago, when he was made permanent, for the partner who never materialised, sipping a sherry and listening to his next article. He imagines her making small criticisms. The domestic image warms him for a time.

Then he remembers that the heating oil is gone, that the house
has been cold for four days, and that he has been heating the
kitchen from the gas oven. That he is sleeping with coats on the
bed. And then there are the noises, the rats, the conversations. It is
as though the house has somehow retained the imprint of previous occupants, human and animal. A spasm of self-pity overtakes
him. When he looks at his watch he knows that yet again the
heating-oil company will be closed. Friday night, another weekend
plunging into the chaos of his private life, the emptiness.

When he made his way to the bookshop he was already half-
paralysed by dread. He stood inside the door for a time, checking
through the recent arrivals, but really just allowing the heat to
soak through him. Then the thought came to him that he should
buy her a book, Hughes' bleak look at the animal of the world, the
survivor.

She wore black too. A crow perched in his memory.

'Closing time, sir,' the girl said.

'Yes, yes,' he said.

'Are you all right, sir?'

He looked blankly at her.

'Are you OK? Would you like a glass of water?'

He handed her the book and fished in his pocket for the money.
A spill of banknotes littered the floor, the table. The shopgirl
gasped. Another girl rushed over and began to pick them up,
brown and blue and green rags rustling in their hands. Their
heads together at the level of his knees.

They were both redheads.

What were the odds? Important to calculate, if only he knew
how. Somewhere there would be statistics. And everything had
significance. There was no such thing as a random occurrence.
No accidents. The girl could be anywhere. She might never come
back again. Or she might. Which was worse?

'There must be five hundred quid,' the shop-girl said.

'Jesus!'

He saw that there was burnt food oozing from the door of the
cooker and a rubble of crumbs and pieces of food: utensils, a mug,
tea-bags and paper on the worktop. How long had this been
accumulating? He wandered around the house, small enough not
to need much time, and saw that the only room that was
habitable was his study, what had originally been the third, tiny
bedroom. Here everything was neat: the wall of books catalogued
according to the Dewey System; the desk with his notes to one
side, a small stack of books he had been meaning to read on the
other, pen and paper in the centre; the chair angled to the desk
the way he liked it. He saw it all suddenly in metaphorical terms.
The study was the empty formality of his lectures, the pointlessness of his academic work. The rest of the house was the filth and
chaos of his private life. Somehow, he knew, the lectures he had
been giving recently were the objective expression of whatever it
was that was destroying him. He even wondered whether the girl
in the black leggings was a creation of a disordered mind, the
scrambled expression of his despair.

'Get a grip on yourself,' he said aloud. 'You're falling.'

Where was he falling? What was he falling into?

His seventh lecture was on disease. He had forgotten his notes,
the leather bag empty and caved-in looking. He stood at the
podium, swaying a little, swallowing frequently. He looked
about him but could not see her. He closed his eyes and began
to speak.

'Pliny,' he said and then recollected that he was supposed to
have moved on, that he was supposed to have come up to the
sixteenth century at least. Where had he been at the last lesson?
Was it Sir Thomas Browne?

'Pliny is a little outside our field of reference for today,' he said. 'But it should be said that he was a firm believer in crickets as a cure for earache. Perhaps anyone with a hangover might like to look up the reference. There's a perfectly good prescription in it, and it's not a controlled drug. First you catch your cricket using an ant tied to a hair . . .'

There was laughter. He had them again. He felt the air cool suddenly, as though someone had opened a door. He remembered the fury of cleaning he had gone through on Sunday night, a kind of purge. The whole house smelled of disinfectant and toilet duck still. This was Tuesday. Or was it Friday? Pliny also favoured the seminal fluid of a boar collected from the sow as it dripped. Mustn't say that. Offensive. Trying to offend again – where does the urge come from?

'*The Anatomy of Melancholy*,' he said. 'Robert Burton, remember? Hamlet? You'll have come across that one in Professor Dawkins' course? Burton says . . .'

He felt unsteady on his feet, uncertain suddenly of the provenance of the quotation he was about to recite. Where did it come from? He was unaware that it was there, crouched in his memory. Was it complete? Would it emerge whole and live in his mind and theirs, or was it to be stillborn?

'The devil, Burton says, being a slender incomprehensible spirit, can easily insinuate and wind himself into human bodies, and cunningly couched in our bowels, vitiate our healths, terrify our souls with fearful dreams, and shake our minds with furies.'

Terrify our souls with fearful dreams. Last night he had dreamed of the girl in the black leggings. He saw her first in her natural shape, the thin face, the shape of her pelvic bones in the elastic fabric. She was very close to him, her face close, and he could smell her breath, her apple-and-coffee air between them. And then she was animal. There was hair on her face and her features had elongated. She opened her mouth and took his penis into it and he ejaculated spontaneously. He looked down and saw her eyes open, ecstatic, the pupils enlarging like saucers. Then she bit down hard and there was blood flowing as copiously as his semen, spurting with the same spasm. Then he was awake and he could not account for the pain in his groin, although the sticky wet of his shorts was plain enough. He lay doubled on his side, clutching his testicles for ten minutes, and when it eased he got up and showered.

He was conscious suddenly of a great pressure of thoughts and words, voices even, crowding his mind, clamouring to be uttered. The words seemed too fast to be spoken. Confusion. Babble. Then Topsell's clear confident prose coughed itself into his mouth and he spoke it as though it was his own. To provoke urine when a man's yard is stopt.

It was pouring out of him now, a torrent of filth. He knew not whence it came, was powerless to stop it. Somewhere in the bleakness of his unconscious he had secreted it, awaiting the propitious time. He felt the importance of the hour, the timely presence of exactly the right words. His voice settled into a chant, sing-song, like a self-conscious poet.

' "To provoke urine when a man's yard is stopt, there is nothing so excellent as the dung or filth which proceedeth from the urine which a horse hath made, being mingled with wine and afterwards strained and poured into the nostrils of the party vexed." Topsell's *History of Foure-Footed Beasts*.'

People were leaving. Through the diaphanous filter of his eyelids he saw their shadows mounting the steps and spilling out through the swing doors. Nun-shapes, abandoning him finally. Others sat on, open-mouthed or laughing openly.

'Urine was also believed to cure ulcers and afflictions of the anus. Take the sweat of a horse admixed with urine and it will cure the belly-ache, the belly-worm and the serpent of the belly. Sirius rising, collect the urine of an ass for leprosy . . .'

He opened his eyes suddenly, alerted by the silence. She was there, the only one left in the fifth row, staring at him. He stared back. There was a burning pain behind his eyes.

'Gangrene of the hands, feet, eyeballs and genitals,' he told her quietly, 'is reported by Thucydides in 430 BC.'

He looked around and saw that there was a chair standing against the wall behind his back. He slumped into it. His face was wet.

She came down the steps and knelt down in front of him.

'You're not well,' she said. Fifteen, maybe twenty people held their breath, watching the comedy. Even the louts were gone. The nuns were gone. Most of the teachers were gone. The people left were mostly girls.

'No,' he said.

'Where do you live? I'm taking you home.'

'No,' he said. 'Filthy. The house is in no condition. No visitors.'

She took his hand and helped him to his feet, led him slowly up the steps and out onto the landing. A small swarm of his students buzzed at the end of the corridor. They fell silent when he came out. He was conscious of their gaze, a kind of awe in it.

'I bought you a present,' he told her.

He opened his bag. Then he remembered the chaos of banknotes on the floor, the shopgirls fussing over him. He saw the book sitting on the counter to the left of the cash register, the pattern it made with the notes, the rectangles curiously echoing each other. Both shopgirls were redheads. The foreigner was talking about Seneca. Thomas Carew addressed a strumpet and concluded that she had once been in a state of grace.

'I forgot,' he said. 'I didn't buy it because it was vulgar.' He wanted to tell her about the signs but he knew she would be suspicious. Hasten slowly, he told himself. Trust no one.

She walked him the quarter-mile to his house, found his key in

the pocket of his jacket and let him in. The smell – Parazone,
ammonia, Jeyes Fluid, furniture polish, fly-spray – was over-
powering.

'Jesus,' she said. 'This place is fucking poisonous.'

She sat him in a kitchen chair and went round opening all the
windows. He stared bleakly at the cooker. In all his cleaning he
had missed the encrusted edges of the doors. Something black had
oozed out at the lower edge, a bevelled lava which here and there
had dripped onto the floor. A dead fly swam in still life, like a
prehistoric insect trapped in amber.

'What's your name?'

'Vanessa,' she said, rolling up her sleeves. Where the elastic
pinched her forearm reminded him of his first dream, the leggings
nicking her thighs. He groaned.

*Vanessa, the ignorance is so great. Thousands of years of it. What have
we known in that time? Between Galen and Harvey there is nothing
but the same invincible ignorance.*

The reproductive system of hares. That innocent creature.

That he had two reproductive systems.

That his pizzle was directed backwards.

That he pissed backwards and copulated backwards.

*That the female hare could carry a child and get a child at the same
time. For the Matrix is yet another animal within us and which is not
subjected unto the law of our will.*

*And snakes. They said that snakes grew of their own volition from
the spinal column of dead men.*

*I feel the burden of it. It is in my head, it has penetrated my cells. I
feel I am sweating it.*

*When you took me home that night I thought you could save me. I
thought I was going mad. I said, stay with me Vanessa, because by
then you had given me your name. You said, no way. I wanted to tell
you that it was all for you, all the words, all the ideas. That I was*

inarticulate was because of you. Not that I could stop talking. But to talk and articulate are not the same.

He sits there, watching her move. He sees in her the lineaments of the animal. She arches her foot when she walks. Her knees bend slightly, elasticity in everything. When she leans over he sees the cleft of her buttocks, a seam in the centre which is not in the cloth. Her scut is there.

Vanessa.

When he begins to talk she is frightened. Her fear makes her face white, dark pools for her eyes.

She is frighted. Let the hare sit, someone said.

If I could stop, I would.

There is a flow to this, a swollen flood.

Bees, they never lapse into love nor bear young by the pangs of childbirth. Virgil, *Georgics*. She is too cold.

Vanessa, save me.

'Got to go now,' she says.

'Vanessa, stay with me.'

'Got to go.'

Fear in her eyes.

He watches her go out. At first he is paralysed. He shivers although the room has warmed. Then he gets out of the chair and picks up his coat. He puts his coat on, counting aloud to sixty. He goes to the door and looks out. He hears her footsteps but does not see her. He closes the door quietly and steps out into the streetlight. He sees her turn the corner far ahead of him. He follows her.

Virgil's voice in my head, lines learned in childhood. The *Aeneid*. Terrible O Queen are the sorrows you command me to revive.

Infandum Reginæ iubes renovare dolorem. How little Latin he has been required to remember. She turns left and is walking along College Avenue. He slows, lightens his steps, hugs the shadows. He studies her gait. She rolls along now, unburdened. No voices in her head, the weight of the past, a thousand years of scholarship in ignorance.

'Don't think of it,' he says and a girl passing, a secretary or a shopgirl on her way home from work, stares at him.

'Fuck you too,' he says, and she hurries on.

Three streets further and they are into flat-land. The tenements are high, fourth or fifth storeys clawing for light over the rooftops of neighbours. Gardens are dead hydrangeas or overgrown bony fuchsia. There are broken windows patched with cardboard. A piece of paper hangs on a cast-iron door knocker: *Mick gone down to Waxy's for a pint meet me there.* There are broken iron railings and gates that have fallen on their hinges and stick half-open. A small smear of vomit against a door.

She comes at last to the corner house on the street. She takes a keyring from the pocket of her jacket and stands under the streetlamp, selecting the right one. Then she puts the key in the lock and disappears inside without looking up or down. He stands under the same streetlight until he sees a light go on three floors up. When she comes to pull the curtains he hurries away.

'They're offering me leave,' he tells the woman on his left. 'On condition I seek medical help. That's why I'm here. Leave, until the end of term, extension through Michaelmas term if I need it. The Prof says I'm too valuable. Can you believe that? My course? Valuable?'

The woman says that she is sure it is valuable.

'Like hell. He's just covering himself. Unfair dismissal, that's what he thinks is valuable. Statutory sick leave et cetera. You can't fire someone for being sick.'

The woman says she should think not.

'No fucking way,' he says. He is feeling excited. He feels he has taken up a cause. For the first time in days there are no voices, driven out by this new commitment.

The woman shuffles in her chair, managing to put a little space between herself and him, and says yes there was no way.

'Not even if you're sick in the head.'

No, not even then. Although maybe if it came against the work. That kind of thing can come against the work. Not like being handicapped.

'You're right,' he says. 'That's why I'm not taking this sabbatical. I'm going to turn up every day. On time. They can fire you for unpunctuality, did you know that? Oh yes, that's how they do it. It's all in the detail, the minutiæ. You have to watch out for the minutiæ.'

The woman says she always watches out for it.

'They get you every time.'

Nasty things.

'Your turn,' he tells the woman when the nurse comes out. 'Make him give you a prescription, otherwise it's just a waste of a visit.'

But when his turn comes he speaks about headaches not voices. He saw instantly that the doctor was in the pay of the university, foolish enough even to display his medical degrees on the walls.

He never mentions the sounds or the voices or his new ability to watch himself from outside.

The doctor peers into his eyes with a light-pen.

After a time Tom says, 'Do you mind?'

'I beg your pardon?'

Tom says, 'I've had enough of this.'

A thousand years of stupidity and then, in the blink of an eye they invent a machine that sees into the mind. A simple pen.

'I'm checking for abnormalities. Behind the eye.'

'Just give me the fucking prescription,' he says.

Behind the eye is my brain. If he could see in there he would read: KEEP OUT NO TRESPASSING.

The doctor backs off. He sits for a moment on the edge of a desk and then stands up again. A nervous man.

'You need something to calm you down,' Tom says.

The doctor laughs uncomfortably. 'No need for that,' he says. 'You just took me by surprise.'

'What about the prescription?'

'Which prescription had you in mind?'

Another trap. Name the specific and you name the disease.

'That's your job,' he says.

Ants are no good. Piss. Pig spunk. Suddenly he is aware of the inadequacy of his scholarship. He cannot recall one thing to make good the broken mind. There is no specific against a fracture in the bond between the world and the way of seeing it. The realisation is a loss of innocence. Tears begin to roll.

'I am going mad,' he tells the doctor. 'I know it.'

The doctor says, 'Now now. It's not that bad.' He rips three large tissues from a box on his couch and hands them out. 'Here,' he says.

'I have to go.'

'Take your time,' the doctor says, but he stands up and opens the door quickly. 'Come back when you feel able to talk about it.'

There are different women in the waiting room. They stare up at him. He wants to tell them to be careful, to watch out for trick questions, not to let him look into them, but the voices have begun again. The pressure from inside is enormous. He feels he is going to crack open like an egg dropped suddenly into boiling water, the yolk and white burbling out at the fissure, revealing everything.

He stands at a bus stop and tells no one that a spermatical

emission equivalent to one drachm is equivalent unto the effusion of sixty ounces of blood and therefore we cannot but think it abridgeth our days. And although he holds his tongue and never utters a sound, the three elderly women stare at him, and a young man with long hair tied back in a pony-tail moves away to the other side of the stop and watches resolutely in the direction from which the bus will not come.

He has five hundred and seventy-five pounds in his pocket and when he takes out the wad of notes the driver coughs into his hand. He gives him a five-pound note and gets the right change. When he sits down he sees the driver watching him in the high convex mirror that allows him to see back along the bus. He notices that the driver is misshapen, grossly enlarged at the top. His eyes bulge like a toad's.

He has been careful to bring the correct papers this time. He stands at the podium in front of a packed lecture theatre. There are students everywhere: sitting in the aisles; sitting cross-legged on the floor in the right-hand corner; standing at the back behind the louts. There is an air of expectancy. He sees that at last the penny has dropped. Ten years.

He begins by saying that the intrinsic value of metaphor is something which should not be underestimated. In mathematics, for example, there are things which cannot be understood except in terms of imagery. He instances fractal geometry, where the constructed image is acknowledged to be no more than an approximation of the reality it attempts to describe.

He smiles. Nobody smiles back.

She is there too. In her usual seat. He leans forward and adopts a conspiratorial air.

'I could tell you things,' he says.

He talks about the recent death of a lecturer in physics. He tells them about the research the man was doing.

'The Theory of Everything. That's what the physicists are after. The Holy Grail they call it. Of course, they couldn't let him get away with it. He got too close.'

He winks broadly and jerks his thumb in the direction of the ceiling.

'They got to him, of course. It goes without saying. All of us are under threat. Constant threat.'

He is wearing a jacket and tie for the first time in anybody's memory, a neatly pressed shirt, trousers with creases. He stands up straight now, almost a military posture, hands firmly at his sides.

'Anybody who got even close would understand everything. He would know about everything. Think about it. The power.'

He coughs.

A colleague has just pushed in past the crush of louts at the door. He stands at the back, arms folded.

'We must be circumspect. So . . . to get back to the matter in hand, and stand by for further updates.'

He takes up his lecture notes and reads carefully:

'A man emigrates from Kerry circa 1965, the date isn't important. This man gets a job on a building site in London.'

He looks up bleakly.

'McAlpine is the company,' he says. He waits for the nuns to write it down.

'The job he gets is night watchman. He's worried about being up all night because in Kerry he never did stay up late because his Mammy wouldn't let him. He asks the lads on the site what he should do. "O bejaze," says one of them, "you'll need a Thermos flask." "What's that?" the Kerryman asks. They explain to him the multitudinous advantages of Thermos flasks, the hot tay in the middle of the night, mushroom soup if you wanted it, etc. The Kerryman says he'll get one and could they say the name again for him. "I'll do better than that," says one of the lads. "I'll write it

down for you." He takes a pencil from behind his ear because he is
an apprentice carpenter and tears a scrap of paper from his *Daily
Mirror* because he votes Labour. He writes: Condom.'

There is a rumble of expectation from the crowd. This is a good
one now, he hears someone say. He smiles up at them. The
colleague is frowning.

'So he takes the chit of paper to a chemist shop that the lads
have pointed out to him. He goes up to the nice girl at the counter
and hands her the note. "What size?" she says. "Large, medium
or small?" '

He pauses and draws a deep breath through his nose. He has
them, he sees that. Why didn't he try this approach years ago? He
screws up his eyes and makes an effort of recognition. It comes to
him that the colleague is Charlie Kennedy. Semi-permanent?
Temporary whole-time? One step down.

' "Well," says the Kerryman. "I'll be on the job all night so I'll
need wan that'll hold about three pints." '

In the uproar he sees the girl, Vanessa, gathering her things.
She mustn't leave, he knows. She mustn't leave before the end of
the lecture because he must speak to her. He signals wildly for the
laughter to stop.

'I could tell you things,' he shouts and the crowd falls silent. 'I
could tell you things.' She sits back down and looks at her
fingernails. He sees that they are painted blue.

'There are spies everywhere, for example.'

He looks up at them, all his confidence gone.

'A thousand years of invincible ignorance and in the blink of an
eye we can see inside someone's brain? What kind of a species
behaves like that? What have we done to ourselves? We who
have gathered the semen of hogs. Who have torn the eye from the
hyena for the invisible stone. Who have traduced the harmless
hare and accused him of the most bestial acts that we ourselves
have practised? Never think, never think we could not have

understood everything a thousand, two thousand years ago. That is the message. All this was not accidental. We are to blame.'

He was shouting. We are to blame. The theatre was deathly silent. Charlie Kennedy stared open-mouthed.

'We are culpable in this as in all things' he shouts. 'I know this. I know it. Don't ask me how. *Infandum reginæ iubes renovare dolorem.*'

'If you sleep with me,' he says looking directly at the girl, 'the people who are violating my head will go away. They could not bear your innocence, your state of grace.'

The crowd gasps. The girl stands up very suddenly and rushes upwards, stumbling on the central aisle. People on the steps move their feet and crush in close to the seats. Along the back the louts lean closer to the wall and watch her as she passes. Charlie Kennedy attempts to stop her, a look of concern on his face, and then changes his mind and steps aside. She goes out through the swing doors with a bang.

'Open the temple gates unto my love,' he recites, his hands at his side, his head thrown back. He is looking up at the roof. 'Open them wide that she may enter in, and all the postes adorne as doth behove and all the pillours deck with garlands trim.'

And then when the door clatters shut he shouts: 'It was suicide! The bastards forced him to commit suicide because he had found the theory of everything!'

Charlie Kennedy has a hand on his arm. 'Take it easy, Tom,' he is saying. His voice is soothing and concerned, but there is a gleam in his eye, sharp as a serpent's tooth. I know that gleam. It is triumph. The bastard is crazy, he thinks. That's another one gone, another step on the ladder. But I have tenure. Not everyone has tenure here.

'Tom, Tom, slow down.'

He strides towards the door, ignoring Charlie Kennedy's hand, ignoring what he says. Some of his notes slip from the cardboard folder and spill onto the floor. He stops abruptly and stares at the pattern they make. He tilts his head to one side as he looks.

'What is it, Tom?' Charlie Kennedy says.

He shakes his head. 'Meaningless,' he says. 'Nothing there.' He turns and goes through the door. 'I mustn't lose her,' he says.

'Tom, leave that girl be,' Charlie Kennedy says. 'It isn't right.'

He knows where she is going. He hardly needs to keep his eyes open. He walks along the edge of the footpath, curious about the sense of elation that has overtaken him. He thinks about it, examines it as a thing in itself. He sees himself turning his elation this way and that like an *objet d'art*, checking its provenance, checking for flaws, for imperfections, for the mark of the maker. He concludes that it is indeed a flawless thing, perfect in itself, something to take joy in.

It's a perfect day, he thinks. That's why I'm happy. And I have declared myself. Two truths are told as prologue to the swelling act. I told her I loved her and I have given out the secret. Now they know that I know. They know that all my years of scholarship have not been for nothing. I have seen into the essential being of things.

He whistles as he walks. He balances on the exact edge of the footpath, his arms extended from his sides like a tightrope walker. Then he begins to dodge the lines on the pavement, stepping only on the unmarked places. He is so absorbed that he does not notice her standing at the gate of her house, watching him.

'Leave me alone,' she says.

He shakes his head. 'I love you.'

'No you fucking don't, you mad bastard.'

'You can't drive me away. I know why you're doing this.'

'You know nothing.'

'You're wrong,' he says. 'I have read widely. But I have terrible dreams. Remember Burton. He had them too, I'm convinced.'

'*The Anatomy of Melancholy,*' she says suddenly. It is as though a light has come on in her head. She looks at him differently, as though studying him really for the first time. 'Come inside. I'll get you a cup of tea. Then we're going to have to call someone. I'm not fucking nursemaiding you.'

They go up the grimy stairs. His hand slides on the banister and he feels the years of chip-fat on the paint, the slime of a thousand students' sweat. The carpet is so worn that the bare boards show through in foot-sized pieces. A board is missing on the first landing and in the darkness below he sees cigarette butts, tissue paper, chewing gum.

'For Christ's sake come on,' she says, catching his arm and pulling him away from the hole.

'Everything is important,' he says, by way of explanation. 'Everything. Most importantly what is discarded. Or appears to be.'

Her flat is one room. An untidy bed in one corner. A two-burner camping-gaz stove on a Formica table, an obscene red rubber tube linking the stove to the scarred blue bottle beneath. A sink. Two chairs and another table by the window. The view is of the concrete garden of the house behind.

She fills a kettle and lights the gas. He sits by the window and sees a clothesline down in the shadows, small things swinging in the cold.

'You're not well.' She is kinder now. When she turns he can see that she is concerned.

'I am not,' he says.

'You should go for help.'

He shrugs. 'What can I do? It's too dangerous.'

'No,' she says, 'that's all in your head. That's just what you think now. If you had help you'd see things differently.'

He looks up at her.

'I feel like a puppy,' he says, 'begging from his mistress for a scrap.'

She folds her arms and leans back against the table with the kettle on it. He has the strange feeling that her body is humming.

'You have to stop saying all those things.'

'I can't. They're in my head. They just come out. Sometimes I don't even think them. Somehow they just . . . appear. My skull utters them but my brain hasn't formed them. Like that.'

She makes the tea and they sit close at the table, husbanding the heat between them, the steam rising in a shaft of bleak sunlight that comes down the valley in the rooftop behind. In the end she sighs and says, 'I can't do anything for you.'

'I know that,' he says. 'I see that.'

'Not for the reasons you think.'

'No. Of course not.'

He says he knows she cannot love him, not after what he has said and done. The enormity of it overwhelms him. He puts the cup down on the floor to use both of his hands. He gestures towards the sky. 'I have gone too far,' he says. 'The things I have done and seen.' She shakes her head. It's not that, she insists. His foot disturbs the cup and it tips over onto its side, the last of the tea spilling out. They watch it spread into the groove of the floorboards. Then she picks up the cup and stands it on the table out of his reach.

'I have a baby.'

He looks around.

'Yes,' she says. 'Here. A friend minds him while I'm at lectures. That's why I'm hardly ever around. I can't bear to leave him for long. That's why I was so angry about all those references. I spent hours in the library looking them up because I thought they were important. I hated you for taking me away from him. I understand now.'

He begins to cry.

'I'm so sorry,' he says.

'It's real for you, isn't it? Not like the others.' She hands him a tissue from her sleeve. It is folded into a neat square. He wipes his eyes but the water continues to flow silently.

'He's six months old today.'

'Is there a father?'

'Of course there's a fucking father,' she says. 'You don't think I did it *in vitro*?'

He shakes his head. 'I meant here.' She shakes her head.

'Fucked off straight away,' she says. 'Good riddance.'

He says he could help. He has money. He has not spent his salary in over a year. His house is full of banknotes. He will give them all to her so she can get a bigger flat.

'In fact' he says, a sly look coming into his eyes, 'why don't you move into my house. I'll sublet a room to you. It'd be a purely commercial arrangement.'

She laughs. 'I'm sure it will.'

'You'll do it?'

She says no, she won't do it.

He gets up and walks around, rubbing his palms together. He says that she will regret it. His house is comfortable, three bed-rooms, a kitchen, a full bathroom and shower, central heating. He's almost never at home because of his researches. He slaps his palms together and his pacing speeds up. He tells her that she is beautiful but that beauty is dangerous. She has power and she must use the power magnanimously. She must yield to him. If he can lie with her and spill his seed into her it will cure his mind. An emission of semen equivalent to one drachm, he tells her, is all that is required. That will relieve the pressure behind his eyes because it thins the blood.

She stands up and goes behind the table. She looks around but sees only his empty mug. She picks that up.

'My baby will be home in a few minutes,' she says.

'Hah! Heard it before. There is nothing new under the sun.'

But just then there is a knock at the door. She rushes to it and throws it open. A red pram is pushed in and a girl follows it. The girl is older than her, more settled-looking.

'Safe and sound,' the girl says. 'Changed, fed and burped. All ready for his mammy. Hello?' she says to Tom. She looks at Vanessa, one eyebrow lifted, the ghost of a leer on her face.

'This is one of my lecturers,' Vanessa said. 'Tom Ryan. He's just going.'

He shakes his head.

'Oh yes you are,' she says.

He sees that the strange girl and Vanessa are aligned against him. They stand and glare. He smiles.

'I see the way it is,' he says. He brushes past them and goes down the stairs two at a time.

He makes elaborate preparations. First he tracks down all the banknotes. He has a shoebox that says Nike Air on the side. He jams the notes into it, squeezing the last few into awkward corners. Then he tapes up the box, running the tape along the edges to make it neat, to seal it down well. He tapes all the corners too, and finally hefts it in his hand. Then he covers the box in brown paper and writes her address on the outside, Vanessa, 18 Boyle Street. He knows he could trace her surname at the Department but feels it might compromise her, leave her exposed. He does not think he should give anything away.

From time to time, as he packs the money, he stops to listen, tilting his head slightly. Always when he does this there is a puzzled look on his face. The voices are silent. He listens for them but they do not come.

Now he scours the kitchen again, cleaning everything. He goes around the house cleaning every surface he might have touched. No prints, he tells himself. They will find nothing. Then he unplugs the washing machine and cuts the cable at the machine end. He separates the three wires and pares them to expose the copper. He cuts away the earth. Then he winds the wire around itself and puts it in his briefcase.

'I want to tell you what has been happening,' he says. He looks up at the tiers and sees Dawkins and Lennon and Charlie Kennedy up there, sitting together at the back. They are staring impassively at the blackboard behind him. On the blackboard he has written FORGIVENESS TIME. He wonders if any of them knows that it is a quotation from a Berryman poem. Also I love him, me he's done no wrong for going on fifty years. Forgiveness time. Probably not. He shuffles his lectures notes and looks down at his own neat script. After this, he thinks, I'm going to buy a computer.

'Pliny,' he says. 'Pliny spoke to me. And our old friend Sir Thomas Browne. Galen. There's an interesting man. I knew him.'

Once again he senses the order and discipline of what he is saying. It seems to him that his words have an intense clarity, like a single intense pinprick of light shining in a deserted landscape.

'Suicide is not a sin. I have it on no less an authority than Seneca.'

There is an audible gasp. Professor Dawkins shuffles uncomfortably and says something to Charlie Kennedy. Kennedy nods and looks at his watch.

'But they have all gone. That is what I wanted to explain. The voices are silent. Can you imagine what that is like? If I say to you that I have had knowledge, you will know what I mean. *Knowledge*. Because you have heard me speak about it. You know my insights. Twenty years of scholarship prepared me for it. A difficult path to follow. Now I am desolate. The voices, the power, the knowledge that I was at the centre. How can I live without it?'

They see him open his briefcase and look in. Some of them lean forward in their seats in the hope of looking into the mouth of the case.

'Come down, Vanessa. Vanessa understands everything. She is an initiate. Come down, Vanessa.'

There are hisses of 'Don't go down, Vanessa' and 'Go down, Vanessa.' A girl sitting near her reaches across two companions and tugs her arm. She says, 'He's crazy, Vanessa.'

Vanessa shakes off the hand and stands out into the aisle. Professor Dawkins stands up too and begins to make his way past the gaping students that sit between him and the aisle. Charlie Kennedy follows.

Professor Dawkins says, 'Stay where you are, young lady.'

Vanessa comes down as far as the second step, no further. He remembers she spoke to him from that step, the first time, the very first time. Significant.

'I sent you the money,' he says. 'You'll be all right now.' He looks up at the crowd. 'Vanessa had my baby,' he says. They stare bleakly down at him. Vanessa shakes her head. 'We did the deed of darkness in her bed. The beast with two backs.' He laughs loudly, throwing his head back a little, letting the muscles in his throat open, a full-throated laugh, a relief. '*Othello*. Iago said it – the beast with two backs. We did. I gave her a baby, now I'm giving her the truth. Come closer, Vanessa.'

'Stay where you are!' Professor Dawkins shouts.

He smiles.

'I won't hurt you.'

Charlie Kennedy climbs over the back of his tier and walks along the tops of the benches. He mounts higher until he is at the back row. The louts standing there part for him and he drops to the aisle. He hurries out and the door slams behind him.

'Too late for security,' he says. He laughs. 'This is the truth.'

He looks down at his notes and realises that after all the order is not there. The letters are random, higgledy-piggledy. He sees individual words. Hog. Slime. Heartsease. Panacea. And names. Pliny the Elder. Aristotle. Burton. He puts his finger down to steady the words and he follows the finger down to the page. If he reads exactly what he has written, he knows, the lecture will return to order. He is aware that there is water on his cheeks. He begins to read.

'God has given you one face,' he says. He notices that it is not what is on the page in front of him, that the words come from somewhere else. 'And you make yourself another. You jig, you amble and you lisp and nickname God's creatures and make your wantonness your ignorance.'

He looks up and sees that a security guard is standing at the top of the hall talking into a radio. Charlie Kennedy is beside him.

'I have tenure here,' he shouts. 'You can't get rid of me as easily as that. You bastards.'

Vanessa says, 'Take it easy, Tom.'

'You said I was lying. You left the baby on his own. What kind of a mother is that? You were trying to check up on me.'

'No,' she says. 'No, someone looked after him.'

'Remember one thing,' he says. 'I know. I *know*.'

What dreams may come should give us pause. I have done the state some service and they know it.

'O rose thou art sick,' he chants, 'the invisible worm that flies in the night in the howling storm has found out thy bed of crimson joy and his dark secret love doth thy life destroy. That's your sex. Remember *The Physiologus*, *The Bestiary*. I have the stone from the hyena's eye. I *have* it.' He stares into her eyes. He puts his index finger to his temple and moves it slowly through the air until it is pointing directly at her. 'It is real.'

'Fuck you!' she shouts. 'Who gives you the right!'

'Don't!' Dawkins calls to her. 'Don't say anything. Don't provoke him.' Dawkins' hands are shaking and his jellyroll face is glistening with sweat.

'You're a bastard,' she shouts. 'You're a sadistic bastard, that's all you are. You and your fucking references. And your fucking failure rate.' Her face is white and her hands too are trembling. He sees that her fingernails are painted black. They are gleaming beetles at the ends of her fingers. When her hands move the beetles ripple.

'Jesus Christ,' he says. 'They were right. Everything is corrupt.'

Charlie Kennedy gapes from the back. Lennon is on a mobile phone. The security man is coming down the steps one step at a time, very slowly. He does not look happy. He has clipped the radio to his belt and in the silence everyone can hear a small sibilant voice saying, 'Mick, come in over, Mick, are you there, come in over.' The security man ignores the voice. He has already stretched one hand in front of him, fingers open, as though anticipating the final lunge. Professor Dawkins is two steps behind him. When they reach the last few steps they push Vanessa to one side very gently. The security man says, 'Excuse me, miss.' The radio crackles again. 'What is he doing now?' the voice says, 'Mick, for fuck's sake gimme something.' The security man looks at Tom.

Tom takes a deep breath . Now is the time, he thinks. Now or never.

'I *know*,' he shouts. 'I'm going to tell you the truth.'

Vanessa will understand, he thinks. And some of the better ones. It will not be wasted on them.

'Take it easy there, sir,' the security man says.

They see him bend down and fiddle with something behind the podium. The security man thinks: Sweet Jesus not a gun. He feels paralysed, unbearably exposed. He hears what sounds like the clunk of a plug inserted in a socket, or a magazine fitting into place.

When Tom straightens again he has a piece of electric flex in his hand, the end pared away, a forked tongue of copper at the end of it.

'Jesus,' the security man says. 'Cut the power.' He unclips the radio from his waist and hisses into it, 'Cut the power in here, for Christ's sake!' The radio voice crackles back, 'Repeat the last message Mick, over.'

'This is the message,' Tom says quietly. He holds the flex in front of his face, the serpent-tongue flashes dull copper at him. 'I still have tenure here,' he says.

He opens his mouth and bites down hard on the wires.

AUGUSTUS YOUNG

The Grandfathers

Mr Sheridan French should be the gentleman half of a Dresden china figurine. Instead he is a court clerk. His courtliness lends the judge authority. Clarion calls for order are moderated by empathic gestures of polite alarm. Unhappy litigants, trembling across the divided court, freeze. Silence sucks in the anger till all is calm. The judge pronounces in a passionless vacuum – judicious words dignified by the echo.

'The defendant is found guilty. Extenuating circumstances (*Your Honour, he was found drunk*). His sentence is . . . to be put on the boat to England.'

'If justice is not seen to be done, it at least can be heard.' Sheridan French intimates this to a callow student over whiskey in the Oyster. The cavernous tavern is famous for its rare steaks and even rarer wines (nobody in Cork can afford them). Etiolated fingers fatten towards the tips, which meet to form a cathedral. He puffs into the sanctuary, hands splay like a priest re-enacting the helplessness of being crucified. 'The best,' Sheridan remarks casually, 'is the enemy of the good. God's on the side of big battalions.' Quotations pepper his conversation like the samplings of today from Late Great Pop idols.

The lady in the Dresden would be tranquil. A haven of good sense, the mantelpiece. Inclining towards her, his phrenologist's dream of a head would hold its own despite its willowy frame. His hair is like a helmet of worms, tufts permed into place. He is clad in court clothes – black jacket with silken lapels and pinstriped trousers, grey tie, ineptly knotted, starch-stiff detachable collar. The stains on his shirt are cloaked by a cardigan. I notice this as the evening loosens his buttons.

Elegance is appreciated for its rarity value in our town.

Sheridan is a night student of my father. He wants to escape. 'The law by day confirms for me that the world is a crook's paradise. I flounder by night in history's quagmire for precedents proving it was always thus.'

He rolls a cigarette. I match it.

'My crooked smoke,' he murmurs, admiring the smouldering thread, 'above the stir of this dim spot which men call earth.'

'Damn spot.' O'Leary has arrived to complete the party. Sheridan ignores him.

'Out of the gnarled timber of humanity no straight thing can ever be made.'

His sentences are patterned by word counts. 'If you can't say something important in fourteen words, better shut up and listen. If you can't shut up and listen, better say something important in fourteen words.' The pauses between are made to count.

This habit, he claims, was inspired by a character in Turgenev who found all great thoughts were contained within fourteen words. He has a store of examples from Pascal, Schiller, Rousseau and Kant. Courts, like war, are boring. Sheridan totted up words in dictionaries of quotations and concluded that Voltaire was the greatest thinker. More of his wisdoms attained the requisite number.

Sheridan's measured discourse is not consistent. 'That's a half-thought, only seven words.' We stopped counting.

His doctoral thesis on Voltaire is slow to develop – ten years old and still not ready to read or write. Stray paragraphs hover with the smoke on the ceiling of the Oyster. Mostly quotes. 'Men only use their thoughts to justify wrongdoing, and words to conceal their thoughts.'

O'Leary – a fellow chronic student – is sympathetic. 'Everything is good leaving the Creator's hands. But goes to bad in man's.' He lost his draft Rousseau thesis on the Circle Line while researching in London.

I sense they are both trying to impress me or impress my father through me. Fat luck. A gargantuan arts student who lives and studies on pints of Guinness in the Oyster glad-waves from his stool. 'Is that lemonade you're drinking, French? Voltaire drank lots of it to cure his smallpox.'

Sheridan dismisses him with a delicate 'phfft'.

'Get back to your books,' hoots O'Leary, 'and earn your Guinness.'

The roused giant is not to be outdone. 'Mock on, mock on, Voltaire, Rousseau. Mock on, mock on, it's all in vain./You throw the sand against the wind, and the wind blows it back again.'

I count the words – it is two word-sonnets.

Sheridan is telling us that 'Voltaire began in the law and ended up an outlaw who dined with Emperors.'

'Just like you, my friend,' remarks O'Leary, 'and that's Nero over there.'

The Guinness giant will get a first-class degree and a scholarship to Montpellier. And die before he is thirty. But in the Oyster that evening the world is his and ours.

O'Leary and myself are invited for a last drink at Sheridan's. He is known to have a little wife at home, a down-to-earth local girl who keeps a stormy marriage pegged to reality. Not that Sheridan would raise his voice or puff the house down. He is a gentleman. The gales all come from the wife. Her frying pan greetings for his tipsy midnight arrivals are legendary. I am curious.

We take a short cut across the fields. Sheridan leads, swinging a cane. Midnight. Full moon. Cows squat like ornaments under a sycamore tree. The river, not far off, freshens the silence. The evening chills – three drunk men hardly notice. Pounding forward with sweaty faces through the clumpy grass. Sheridan waxes lyrical about my father, intonation lowered. O'Leary is nodding agreement. All the irony and scoffing of the evening ('Not having succeeded in the world, they took their revenge speaking ill of it') drained to a reverential hush. I am disappointed, wanting the low-down on my father. It's embarrassing. Could it be their careers depend on it? Unworthy thought.

The hedge surrounding the fields is fuchsia. I tear a flower off and say, 'Dancing Pavlova. That's what he calls them. Now tell me one bad thing about the Professor.'

Sheridan stops dead. Looks at me. His aristocratic face is gothic, demonic. 'One thing I can't stand about your father. At social gatherings. He accepts a drink, a small whiskey. And barely touches it all evening. I can't keep my eyes off the glass. Half full when he leaves. I always make a point of finishing it.'

He does not count his words. This is serious.

The last field is barbed-wired. Sheridan raises it with his cane and ushers O'Leary and myself through. But stays put with the wire outstretched.

'What are you doing, French?' O'Leary exasperates.

'It's the grandfathers. I'm letting them through.'

Midnight. Moonlight. Three drunken men stand by while their respective grandfathers pass through the hoop. Six grey eminences honoured. I think of mine. Never knew either. They died before I was born. I missed them. Now Sheridan has gifted me two grandfathers, if only for a minute. I hear the river. French's house is by the weir.

A three-room cottage. Mrs French opens the door. Three drunk men. She is tiny and homely, no Dresden. Pleasant enough in her annoyance.

'The boy is asleep. We can't invite your friends in.'

Sheridan remonstrates gently. Then slides to the ground, his cane breaking the fall. We pick him up.

'I know you. You are . . .' Mrs French steers the lifting party to a chair where Sheridan is perched. 'The Professor's son. I don't mean to be unwelcoming.'

'He needs his whiskey,' confides O'Leary, 'and a good sleep.'

We leave.

'Jeremy Bentham's clothes-horse corpse sitting in state in London University,' O'Leary hoots.

Sheridan's thesis was eventually published. The *Times Literary Supplement* approved. 'Mr Sheridan French has written an elegant book about Voltaire.' Like Gibbon after completing *The Decline and Fall of the Roman Empire*, he settled for walks, talk and whiskey. ('The superfluous is a very necessary thing in the best of all possible worlds.') Two years before retiring from the History department, he was granted tenure. My father was with his own grandfathers by then.

His son – like Voltaire in his wilderness years – moved to London. He has his father's hands. Plays the violin in the Harrow Philharmonic.

Sheridan French's grandson is called Candide.

MARY LELAND

The Purple Dahlia

At Inishannon the road was flooded as she drove through the village, copying the caution of the cars in front, the cars behind. The countryside lurked between shrouds of rain. She wondered how the Bandon river would look at the bridge near Ballinadee – no swans now, and the green hairy streamers abandoned in the wash. If the road was impassable there would be warnings, surely? She should be safe, in any event, if she kept to the high centre line. Now she was safe in the cave of the car, everything in working order, heating, wipers swiping the cascades across the windscreen, dims on, de-mister demisting, the tyres firm and thick and sending breakers of water back into the drenched ditches.

The radio was efficient: scores from Lansdowne Road and Old Trafford and St James's Park, the voices excited. The gloom held down by the cloud was pierced by analysis, own goals, tries, new signings, sendings off. A triumph over hurdles. And by music – well, songs of the day, or of the hour. In the glove compartment – yes, gloves – and a torch and the mobile phone. Better put that nearer, on the passenger seat.

The burdened St Christopher swung over the rear-view mirror. How had he got there? Who knew about St Christopher these days? It was a song, wasn't it, something her daughter's friend had heard about the saint, a road song, like a road movie? And because of all this travelling the girl had found the little figurine and installed it there, not an act of faith so much as an act of affection. It was something to be liked by one's children's friends.

But there was this ache at her back. In her back, there to the right of the spine where the cushion had slipped. She steadied herself against the seat-belt and twisted one shoulder away from the other, twisting one hip away from the other, careful as cars dredged past in the other direction, trying to make her deliberate movement balance the instinct to dodge the spray. It was a trick to shift in her seat without lifting her foot from the pedal and there was so much slowing down to do here where the verges were ponds and the crown of the road the only highway. It took concentration, this movement away from pain. It was a distraction from the simplicity of deluge and danger, from squinting between the blades of the wipers and their slashed, interrupted orbit around the narrow world.

This wasn't a muscle ache. She knew that when she would get out of the car in Kilcrohane, when she had swished through the rivulets of all those peninsulas, by then more than one muscle would be aching, there would be a stiffness in her right leg from its purchase on the accelerator. She would suffer precisely the consequences of sitting too low too long. No – this was different. It was like – gosh, she smiled to think of it – it was like when she had periods, that premonitory tension which was all the trouble she had ever had in that department but which when it came was accurate and unyielding. The only thing that had matched it – and this had been a surprise, the things people never told you! – the only comparable sensation was the warning of contractions before the births of her children. Yes, that sensation of something already wound tight being tightened further, a soreness, almost like pressing deliberately on a wound, a pain that was thin, vein-like, or like a stem with a flower of blood on it, the blossom contained until it had to break into its fullness of meaning. Travail, she thought, now that she could think of these things as past. From the French, *travailer*, to work, to labour.

Not to travel. *Voyageur* is the traveller. And why, as she

travelled, was this travail come upon her? She peered into the world beyond the windscreen and met the composed saint, staff in one hand, the child on his shoulder. As she remembered it, there was a river to be crossed and Christopher carried the child Jesus through the flood. That was a journey too, of sorts. In a way, she thought, we are all Christophers, carrying our children through what may be coming to meet them. And when was that going to stop? She thought of his morning's telephone call. 'Don't tell me another word about him!' she remembered saying. 'I don't want to meet another boyfriend – or girlfriend for that matter – for as long as I live!'

There were protests down the line. No-one was promiscuous. She would have preferred it, she said, if they were. 'Or else get engaged!' she had said. 'Get married, set up house together – I don't care. But don't introduce me to anyone else. I don't want to like and feel for and care about anyone new – and then, after six months or twelve, never see or hear of her again!'

St Christopher eddied across her sightline as she remembered the telephone telling her she would have to cool it, to get real. This was good advice, she knew. These young people weren't abandoning one another when they moved on, or so they said, and so they believed. But she had seen the tears of the left behind, the grief and bewilderment of those, even these very children themselves, when they had been the ones moved on from. No, they said; they said no, now on the telephone, or on their visits home when a new name was dropped into the conversation, or on her visits to Paris, or London, or Boston when a different presence was announced and for ever a statue – that magnificent king, Clovis, wasn't it? In Paris near Nôtre Dame? Dripping with verdigris? – or a restaurant or a river – Oh, the Vlatava that time in Prague – such things, such places became inseparable from a smiling guest whose smile was taken to her heart and grew there during months of constancy. Like a little pregnancy. She could not read the genetic map, she could not tell when the miscarriage would bleed through the month's news.

In the meantime there would be Christmas cards. There would be home visits and the pushing together of beds in the guest room. The rattle of pill packets in the guest bathroom. There would be gifts, and little kindnesses, and the name repeated in the details of a holiday or a weekend away (away! Ski-ing, that might be, or a *gîte* in Provence, or a hunting lodge in the mistiest, most purple pages of *The Hidden Ireland*!) or a dinner in the apartment.

As the road disguised itself in a river she thought of the end of the telephone call, the weekend call which kept her in touch just as they forwarded their important e-mails although she knew there were plenty of these not forwarded to her and that was a good thought, that they wrote to and telephoned one another without any reference to her, they were their own people now and liked one another.

Is this what happens? Is it that she has no capacity for love? Not that she cannot love: she has loved, does love, fiercely and consistently. But not flexibly. As if her emotional muscles, the pelvis of her spirit, could not be stretched beyond the span of sinews weakened by pain. There is no room for more, no space for that other kind of love which is no less honest for being volatile. She did not express this very well this morning on the telephone. And when she said she was about to set off on this journey, on a day such as this, and said her goodbye so carefully as if all the love of her whole life could be parcelled and transmitted down the line, she knew that the message was decoded. To the adult child she was saying: your loving mother whom you may never see again because she is driving off to work on a wicked day wants you to know that you have been the most wonderful children any mother could have had and have been the greatest happiness and reward of her life.

Ah, had mocked her daughter who, astonishingly, had been

reading Harold Nicolson, *'l'adieu suprême des mouchoirs!'* That's love too, though, isn't it? she questioned herself as the brown rain broke in swathes across the roof, the windscreen. She had no fear that anything was going to happen to her, but she understood only too well the arbitrariness of death and how immensely worse things could be when death left unfinished the business of the heart. On the telephone this was understood. It was always understood, although they grinned from time to time as though they thought it was an unnecessary caution, for what could possibly be going to happen to her?

Little do they know, she thought as the car rocked under her and the wheels cracked the branches strewn on the road. Steady again, she pulled at the cushion behind her back and changed into top gear to get this bit of wood-rimmed highway past as quickly as possible. If that was the safest thing to do? Perhaps all the branches that had been likely to fall had fallen already – or perhaps it was best just to speed away under the trees so that whatever might fall wouldn't fall on her? God!

And today of all days she was visiting a garden. It would be a swamp – although to the south, the radio said, the storm was clearing, the wind was driving westwards, Leinster was in for a bad time, but here, when she craned her neck like a tortoise so she could see some distance ahead, she thought there might be a streak of blue through the cloud.

'You say it best,' sang the radio, 'When you say nothing at all.' Perhaps. She should let some things just be given. Or perhaps her aversion was a reflex, inbuilt as an adhesion from an old wound, having been one of the abandoned herself. Her intolerance, then, could be explained as an affinity. She could not be melodramatic about it, it would be like Cynara – for I am sick of an old passion, I have been faithful to thee, Cynara, in my fashion. Faith and faithfulness. It could be that these were her watch-lights, the widening beam of her lighthouse.

Bandonbridge and the swerve southwards. Familiar roads made threatening only by the weather. She rather liked it, the weather. Something to deal with. And the country out there defying her, denying its greens and ambers, pretending the smoking gold of the furze was quenched when she knew as the woods bent and swayed above her that it was there, held down by cloud and cold, but it would kindle again on the cliffs beyond Kilbrittain. She must not sigh, now that the rain diluted the solid shapes of hotels, houses in preposterous places, the architectural agony of a country at war with its own hinterland. She would let this go, for this journey she would not indulge her urge to protect the fields, the hills which were still unmasted, the trees still actively claiming their right to charm, to shelter or to kill her.

It was time, surely, for her to let the landscape protect itself. To admit that it had grown up. Dank as it was, blown and tattered as it was, what was certain was that it would emerge, resistant, revived, radiant. She had seen it so many times. It would always happen. It might happen differently, but it would take place. There would be, surely, other guardians? 'Let it be, let it be,' sang the radio. Let it be.

Let them be. She settled the cushion again, wondering why she had never taken out that kind of buttoned thing people put against the back of the seat and which, presented with it, she had put in the boot. It was still there. She would take it out at Kilcrohane and tie it on and see if it made a difference to this discomfort. Although there was this much to be said for pain – it kept you awake. At those childbirth classes, she remembered – how seriously she had taken all that kind of thing – at those classes the notion was to welcome the pain, to take control of it and guide it to its fruition. Embrace it. But motherhood was not like that. Welcome, guidance, even control, yes; but fruition was evanescent. Its meaning changed. For her, for years, it had meant only survival. Embrace the pain – it was like love, a capacity which could only be measured as it happened.

That was where the intolerance came from, Cynara, an old wound. She was past those times, they all were, they had not been submerged, not drowned. But it was no wonder she was frightened. Her soul remembered the pain just as her body had its memories. Separation, parturition. And perhaps she had been too stern with herself. She hated exaggeration except for the sake of comedy. She had offered the children no excuses, no-one to blame, although she discovered that they had come to their own conclusions. So they had not mourned together as perhaps they should have done. They admitted grief, shared it, but disguised it. It masqueraded as defiance. As constipation. As this syndrome or that, as music or beards. And they grew out of it, or became accustomed to its weight, although it was a burden that made the heart swell out of shape. Like St Christopher's humped shoulder, his misshapen staff.

For who could tell which, among the injuries of childhood, leave the deepest scars? Who can decide when change is not the metaphor for damage? There had been moments when love and guilt had coagulated in her heart; they surged up now like the road's wet sweep under a breaking shelf of trees. The shuddering shamed tears of the twelve-year-old when the tom cat had killed the cherished new-born kitten. Or ten years later, that dragged-out evening at Moscow airport when delayed luggage kept her incommunicado behind a stolid bureaucracy; he had remained there at the meeting point, weary with expectation, the purple dahlia bought hours before to welcome her with radiance wilting in his patient hand. It had revived, she had told him, in water in her hotel room. Its delicate white stripes shone on her window ledge. It was the pledge from his world to hers. She could not let it die while with him she walked the city and tried to love it, or at least understand it, as he did.

These were not tragedies. Worse things had happened, so much worse, for other people, and she remembered that newly-opened grave beside the path into the church. In the country way it was lined with laurel and wintersweet as if to make its eighteen-year-old tenant more welcome, more comfortable. No, she thought, I and mine have been lucky. So far.

Yet this drag as she drove onto the southern archipelagoes was like a revenant. A phantom of an ache which once had meant something more than just itself. Not a wound so much as a process, an event, and rain wrapped around it somehow, and damp underfoot and trees lowered by their skein of mist and her car raking leaves and gravel together under the wheels. The house squat and solid and its small windows without light and the rain drumming on the glass roof of the porch and she with her burden of news to tell to her friend who would not want to hear it, it was too soon, too sudden.

She was there, Mandy, in the house, her car was near the door which was open for the convenience of the cats. But there was no answer to the knocker, to the rap upon the shuttered windows. Again and again, with spaces between each call, each blow on the door or glass, the air left empty for those within the house would not admit the messenger outside. They could not have known what she came to tell. This was a kind of anguish that drove her breath in gushes to hang on the air. The sea mist sulked below the hill, as if too swollen to climb up this far, and the village looked so faint and distant – whom else could she call? Knock and call, knock and call, she was shouting now, rattle the latch on the scullery door, walk behind the house to see nothing, not even a flicker of light, unearthly – why the darkness? Could they already know?

But the house breathed in long sighs like the sea. It was inhabited. She was there, Mandy, within it, stealthy. It was time to march in, to lift the scullery latch and enter the dark. As she

152 MARY LELAND

grasped the handle of the door it opened on a thick screech and
Johnny stood there, and said as if taught to say foreign words that
his mother was not in. No, he had said again and then again, no.
Mandy isn't here. The lie had lasted through all these years, his
borrowed lie. 'I must speak to her,' she said, 'it's important.' But
no, he said, Mandy isn't home. And then in a tone of forlorn
defiance he said, 'Tell me; I'll take the message.'

It was all wrong. She could feel the wet curls of hair on her
neck as she stood outside a house she would normally have
entered on a welcome, without ceremony, with a hug for Johnny.
She moved towards him now but he stiffened, and she thought –
he's only fourteen. And then she thought – Mandy wants this.
Johnny is only doing what Mandy wants him to do although she
cannot know why I'm here, what it is I have to tell. 'It's
important,' she said again to Johnny. 'I know she's there – please
tell her I must see her.'

'No,' he said. Could he have been afraid? He was ashamed, she
could see that, that was the measure of the lie. She gave in. All
right, she had said. 'It's your father,' she said slowly, making the
words heavy so he would not escape what was happening. 'He
has died. Your uncles wanted you and your mother to be told. If
you get her for me now I can give her more information.'

In the dusky silence his eyes were lowered. She saw how the
close-cropped black hair was like down on his scalp, she could
see, she thought, the tender escarpment of the fontanelle. Caught
in the web of the lie he could not abandon it and get his mother's
help. He had met his father three times in his life, but two of those
times had been in the past few months, and deliberate. A chosen
coming together. Who could know what hopes came to an end
on this death? Those last meetings – what had they bred in this
boy?

'Well,' she said, 'I will write down a telephone number for
Mandy. And when she comes back give it to her, or ask her to

telephone me.' She was trying to anneal the truth by accepting the untruth. And still she could not enter the house. She asked him to sit in the car with her but he refused. He took the piece of paper slowly as if its numbers were a code he could not decipher. He stood there holding it while it got damp and the ink softened.

'Johnny,' she said.

He looked up at her. 'I hope you don't think I mind,' he said. 'He means nothing to me.'

A long time ago. The road to the left of Bantry ran over moorland, fewer trees to worry about although the wind shook the car, she could feel the pressure pushing her towards the verge. Hard shoulder, she thought; hard cheese, the children used to say of one another. The calcium debate, trying to give them good teeth without braces although Johnny, she remembered him saying ruefully, had been wired for sound. The telephone call had come, all that was proper had been done, but there had never been any reference to that visit, to her vigil in the rain outside the furtive windows. It had stained the friendship which yielded in the end to geography. We were all adrift then, she thought. We could only do what we had to do by instinct, by feel. There were no patterns for us to follow. Johnny and her children were allies for a while through being fatherless, but had moved on to different schools, different colleges and now to different countries. And so, she had lost touch.

On the radio a presenter was forecasting his coming programme of old favourites. His father's choice. For example, he said above the surge of rain:

The little toy dog is covered with dust, but steady and staunch he
   stands.
The little toy soldier is red with rust and his musket moulds in
   his hands.

Time was when the little toy dog was new and the soldier was
*   passing fair.*
That was the time when our little boy blue kissed them, and put
*   them there.'*

What had she done to deserve this? Inherited tears blurred her
eyes. Time to switch over, and she found Lyric FM and a trumpet
voluntary to stiffen her spine. The words adhered from remembered childhood, her mother singing to draw sobs from a stone,
the image of the little boy dead in his sleep and the toys left
undisturbed and waiting through the years – steady and staunch,
still in the same old place, awaiting the touch of a little hand, the
smile of a little face. The very worst Victorian sentiment, the curse
of Little Nell, the ideology of infant death. And yet how powerful
that easy sentimentality! Perhaps it had a function; it shook grief
down into tears, into release and that tired acceptance necessary
for survival in a world where infant deaths were commonplace.

Now they die just when we think we've made it. She felt the
softening of the wind as the road wound down from the plateau.
Soon she could decide whether or not to make the detour which
would give her the view of Roaring Water Bay. For her soul's
sake. Perhaps it would be better to press on, although the clouds
were breaking and the rain was drifting into mist, a shaft of light
connecting earth and sky like a Renaissance painting. That was
one thing she had never accepted about the Annunciation; she
could not understand, as she listened to the Magnificat, why
Mary had been so acceptant. Why she hadn't said – living in the
world she lived in, knowing the life she knew – 'Hmm. But what
will happen to him?'

Her messenger, of course, was a harbinger of birth, not death.
But if she had been told of the crucifixion would Mary have
agreed?

The little toy dog. Its evocation of expectation, and of loyalty. It made her weep now because she had been thinking of the purple dahlia drooping in Moscow's airport. Of the passive patience she had imposed on her own children, as it had been imposed on Johnny. If they had learned fidelity, and practised it, and understood its obligations, where had the example come from? She must not examine her life too closely as she wrestled with the weather and the work waiting for her, but she thought of other women, her friends at the tennis club and how in summer she saw those competent bodies, producers of healthy children, yet here in the short white twirl of skirts with the slashing backhand or the fierce two-handed cross-court drive, combative and, for this short engagement, guiltless.

After Durrus she took the longer, higher road and then the Atlantic obliged her with sun on its scattering of islands. Beyond them to the west more clouds threatened the horizon. Mozart flowed in sonatas of consolation from the dashboard and the wipers folded to the brimming rim of the windscreen. Bracken and furze cloaked the hills and cows scratched against the signs offering sites for sale. Arrived at the gate, the avenue, the house, the host with his Labradors, she settled into her job and pulled on the wellington boots and plastic jacket to walk the sodden land. It would be the site of a county-wide festival of arts in early summer. She would describe its shrubs, its double herbaceous borders, its loggia and summerhouse and walled kitchen garden, its conscious reinstatement of lost features, its painstaking recovery of drains, of heating vents in the rebuilt glasshouses. It was charming, commendable, on the high moral ground of modern gardening. Her prose could be loyal to this landscape: it had nothing to hide.

She was offered tea, but said no, she would like to drive around for a while now that the rain had eased and the sun might appear again. But he said, if she had time to spare, perhaps she might like to see another garden? He would just ring to check someone would be there to show them the place, it was quite unusual, she might like it.

It was a fairytale. Explained as a piece of gardening history it was a *cottage ornée*: thatched, deeply eaved, balconies of rustic fencing, reached by a timber bridge over a stream emerging from the clustering woods which opened only here and there to little glades of lawn or shrubbery. She was brought in, made welcome by a group of young men whose whippet bitch, Sophie, was chased from a chair by the fire so she could sit on it. They wore pigtails and earrings although Bird, the only girl, was unadorned, her blonde straight hair hanging to her shoulders. On the ledges of the latticed windows were computer monitors, modems, printers, a fax. They worked in the forest, they told her. A tree survey, and the felling required as a result. And on some of the old gardens overgrown along the peninsulas, the lost gardens which they were clearing according as the grants or the commissions came in.

And here, of course, there was so much to do here. They made tea for her; she accepted tentatively until she saw how the tallest of them, the one who commanded the dog, took the trouble to warm the pot, and used leaf tea, and found a strainer, and milk in a jug. Whose children were these, she wondered, sitting with their booted feet on the arms of their chairs, washed in the leaded sunlight as they explained that their talk of toil meant Time Off In Lieu, serving tea in china mugs from a china tea-pot with a cosy of quilted embroidery?

It was the tallest of them, Sean, who took her outside. He showed where the clearances provided more space, how he mulched and supported his own plantings, how he gathered them so that they sheltered one another. Some were rare, exotic, but here with the Gulf Stream they should have a good chance of surviving. That was how gardens such as this had been built since the eighteenth century, with seeds from expeditions, with transplants from Kew. He had been abroad and had worked in forests in South America, in India, in Canada. He brought her to a view of the dell in which the cottage had been built, showing its place in the ecology of this oak wood on the mountain. They tramped up a squelching hill, Sophie following at heel. He wore his hair in thick black curls and his skin was dark, unusually weathered for one so young. He was glad to be back here.

He had known it as a child, this enchanted place. It had been built for a mad lord from the great estate nearby whose fantasy it had been until he was too crazy to live here any more. Then it was sold and bought and burned down and rebuilt and now at last here he was!

He seemed to think she would know how it had happened and of course she could imagine it. She watched him as he talked. How handsome he was and yet how familiar, some other woman's child brought to this fruition, she felt as if somehow he belonged to her because he was born so successfully of woman as her own had been. And it seemed too that he felt some similar recognition, he was so easy with her, so unaffected, explaining at one moment, listening at the next, sharing his islanded retreat as if she had some right to it.

He was mapping the land now; there was much more of it than appeared around the cottage. There was so much to excavate from the undergrowth that he needed to write a catalogue before he could begin the formal restoration programme. It would take years, he thought, but it was calculated, he and his mates had worked out the price-earnings ratio and how to express the sweat-equity on the commissioning balance sheets. After that he would travel again, but with some security, with a place to come home to.

'It was a risk, I suppose you'd think,' he said. 'When Philip offered it to me, I couldn't say it was the place I'd want to spend all my life. I still can't say that. But it's a good place to start, isn't it?'

It was no trouble to agree. Who, she asked, thinking that she should know the owner of a garden such as this – who is Philip?

'Philip?' He stood to look at her. 'My uncle Philip, of course. I thought you knew Philip?'

He said, 'I thought that was why you were here.'

He seemed to blush, as if anticipating her embarrassment. 'He is, he was, my Dad's brother. I thought you knew him. I thought you knew me.'

To her silence he added: 'You might remember me as Johnny.'

He did not move away from the hand she held out to him. She saw him in this mist of green, in the glade of woodland, the rattle of the stream in her ears. The dog, Sophie, was sitting on the grass at his feet. Smoke from the chimney lay low across the steaming thatch. Her feet in the rubber boots were clenched to hold steady against the slide of the hillock. She could not have been waiting for this moment, but it felt like a moment she had been awaiting all the years since the evening she had first met Johnny, the slender shells of the fontanelle pulsing under his black birth curls.

'I didn't really change my name,' he said. 'It was just later, at school, when I was going to the Gaelteacht to get my Irish right, I used Sean there and I just never changed it back.'

He added: 'Nobody seemed to mind.'

She could not take her eyes off him. There was that slant of the eyelids, more pronounced now against the adult cheekbones where as a child there had been the thick fringe of lashes. There was the lift of the chin, the solidified shape of the bone which then had seemed rounded under the skin. And when he dropped his eyes, as if to spare her any apology, she saw him then, sullen and silent and helpless beneath the wet trees around his mother's house.

If her capacity for love was inflexible, her capacity for pain could always expand. She could embrace it. The glade darkened and rain fell again, and not lightly. They turned back to the cottage, Sophie picking her way at Sean's heels. There was an offer of more tea, food, the young men gathering their debris off the table to prepare an evening meal, the girl Bird sitting at the fire with a skein of wool on her lap and her fingers busy with knitting-needles.

They spoke of the work to be done before spring as cloth, bread, butter in a dish and all the paraphernalia of dinner time began to dress the table. She made her farewells as they interrupted the lists of choisya and myrtle to shake hands with her as if they regretted her departure. They returned to the ordering of their lives. Her first host was staying on and it was Johnny who walked to the car with her.

He agreed that the weather was closing in and she should go while the going was good. He stood on the greensward and looked at the lowering sky and the dusk it was dragging down with it. At least the wind had eased, he said, but as she looked at him the breeze lifted the locks of his hair, spreading them back behind his skull, and his bare profile was exposed, both child and man revealed in this face of today – the boy she had known, the old man she would never know.

She was some miles along the road home before she felt again that tension at her spine. On the radio the news spoke of havoc in flooded villages, a death from a fallen tree, another where a car had driven into a bursting stream. She must be careful, there were miles to go and it would be dark before long. But it was not dark yet. The outline of the sea sharpened the headlands she was leaving behind. The fork at Durrus led her back on a whim to the shore of Dunmanus Bay. She pressed down the window to hear the crash of the sea on the coast's edges. She sucked in the dripping air. She saw where the trees leaning into the land were scalped. In the cold she felt alive. She thought of that girlfriend, wearing to the parting dinner – meagre on a student budget – the gallant dress she had planned for the university ball she would never attend. She thought of one of those boyfriends, hailing her one morning, kissing her, but having nothing much to tell of his life since they had known one another.

She thought of the snow in Moscow, the snow illuminated by sunlight, harsh and unremitting. She thought of the flower at the airport, the dark hue of its petals streaked with white. And gardens, she thought: we work away at our lives, at our gardens, content to forget that they are part of an ecosystem controlled by elements far beyond ourselves, careless of ourselves. A storm is a good reminder. She straightened herself against her seat. She had forgotten to take out that back-support thing. Arthritis, the doctor had mused when she had complained that her stretch at tennis was hindered by the ache. Well, she said to St Christopher as she turned the key in the ignition, she would play on.

FIONA GARTLAND

Vodka on Sunday

When I recall that Sunday afternoon it is a hazy dream bathed in late summer sunshine. Light plays on the crystal lamp, throws rainbows on to the green-painted wall and catches the edge of my mother's glass. She is holding it up and slightly away from her, as if to toast our boldness. There is an intimacy in the way we sit together on the couch, at either end, both with our feet up and facing each other, so that I can see the dried skin of her soles beneath her tan nylon. Dad is gone to Parnell Park, we've opened the cabinet without him and begun a small conspiracy.

Our drinks of vodka and lemonade are warm without ice. The mixer is from a giant bottle of T.K., flat and sickly sweet. But I sip it with pleasure. It reminds me of days when I was little and drank orange beside her. I could never understand why her small drink lasted so much longer than my tall one.

'You got a good colour yesterday,' she says. I had been to the beach and toasted myself nicely. 'You have a brown line across your nose like when you were small.'

We talk at random and what I remember are unrelated subjects, like letters drawn from a Scrabble bag, but it mustn't have been like that. There must have been coherence, some chronology in our ramblings.

'Your father worries about you.'

She says this after she has refilled our glasses and settled herself again on the couch. I pay no attention; it is she who is the worrier. She is the one who sobbed into her hanky the night I was sixteen and Dad caught me kissing my boyfriend at the foot of the drive.

'You were wrapped around him!' Her voice had stretched tight as a rubber band. 'Have you no respect for yourself?'

I'd cried too, with the humiliation of it. Dad said nothing, only clinked the milk bottles. The boyfriend barrelled home.

Her lips come away from the glass. 'Your father's afraid you're too much like me.'

'And what's so terrible about that?'

She's all right for a mother, in fact I'm sneakingly proud of her. She has something, an effect on people. At parties she sparkles like someone's sprinkled her with glitter. She isn't even my mother then, just Nina.

'I'd trust you with my life, do you know that?'

God, she trusts me. I'm not sure at all that I can be trusted, I'm not sure I want to be trusted. In the dark with my boyfriend, his breath hot against my cheek, my passion strains at a thin thread of guilt and fear.

'No matter what happens, you can always tell me.'

Can I? Can I tell her everything? How could she understand, a woman of her time?

'But what if I did something awful?' Awful, awful, wonderful, good, too good to stop, stop, we better stop.

'Like what?' The question comes forward gently, hovers in the air between us, tests our intimacy.

'What if I fail my exams?' The response is lame. She withdraws the question, registers her disappointment.

'Sure, couldn't you repeat those?'

More words float and bounce. She talks in snippets about her childhood, nine children in a two-bedroomed house. 'And always the women doing for the men. I remember my brothers kicking ball on the road while I made their beds. And my mother clipped me round the ear and asked me how I expected my brothers to sleep on that mess. I swore I'd never do that to mine.'

'Oh yes, I remember when you taught Liam to fry an egg. I suppose you can't change the world in one generation.'

'Don't be so smart.' She tips her head back and drains her glass. 'Will we have another little one before your dad comes home?'

She smiles at me, her wide smile that draws her lips up over her teeth and shows the pinkness of her gums. She takes my glass and twists herself off the couch, stretches her legs. She has good legs, neat ankles, slender calves, not dumpy or puffy like so many of my friends' mothers.

'You must have been whistled at when you were young, Mam.'

'Oh now, I'm not beyond the whistles yet.' She laughs and hands me my drink. I swallow and feel the warmth of the liquid reach the tips of my fingers and draw hot patches on my cheeks.

'To this day I'll never know why your father asked me to dance.' She begins to tell a story that is for me as safe and comforting as a lullaby.

'I was standing with Gina at the far wall. The dance hall was packed but I had him spotted. Over he came. He was handsome. And Gina had the most gorgeous frock. She always had the best. I was wearing some dull oul' thing. But he asked me, all the same.'

Of course he asked her. I'd seen the photograph from Rosse's studio: even in black and white she was radiant.

'We'd have to race home after a date, beat your Auntie Betty to the parlour, otherwise we'd be stuck on the stairs for a court.'

A court, a cuddle, the euphemisms of her youth. No question, then, of passion getting out of line.

'It was easier then though wasn't it? Good girls didn't.' I blurt out the words. Feck it, it was easier for her, it must have been.

'Human nature has always been the same.' She doesn't look at me and I'm suddenly unsure.

'I wish I'd known you when you were just yourself, Mam, before you had kids an' all.'

'I was a lot like you, I suppose, not as much sense.' She couldn't have been a bit like me. She never put a foot wrong. She still believes what she hears from the pulpit.

'Did I ever tell you about the nuns?'

'What nuns?'

'I spent a while in a convent, lovely and peaceful it was.'

She wanted to be a nun! The idea horrifies me. I'm still struggling to separate Sister Mary from Vlad the Impaler. She must have been very good then, when she was young, a very good person.

'Why did you leave so?'

'I went home to your Nana's for a visit and they seemed so poor, I couldn't go back, got a job then, in the post office.'

They'd been poor. I didn't know poverty, only caution, the quartered apple and the wet potato skins packed on the fire to stretch the coal. I think of this but don't mention it to her.

She is dreaming again.

'I feel sorry for you with no proper dances, discos aren't the same at all, there's no skill in them.'

I have a vision of her waltzing with Dad, restrained romantic one-two-threes round the floor. I lurch. I drape myself on my boyfriend's neck and shuffle in time to Eric Clapton. He kisses me and we sweat.

She puts her hand to her mouth. 'God, look at the time. Your father will be home soon. I think we need coffee.'

I see that she's laughing when she says this but I don't see her clearly, it's like looking through a Vaselined piece of glass, she is soft at the edges and fuzzy.

'Coffee,' I say.

'Yes, go and put the kettle on.'

The kitchen is a long way off. My legs are heavy. I find the kettle and cups, add the instant coffee powder. The work top is showered in fine brown snow.

'It's on,' I say. I drop heavily into my place, lift my leaden legs on to the couch.

'It's a pity you gave up your dancing, you could have been a teacher.' She touches my toe. I shrug. I never thought of dancing as a career, I never thought of anything. It was she who got me into college. She phoned half a dozen institutions to find a course that matched my meagre points, while I floundered. She got me into Cathal Brugha Street. It didn't seem to matter much after that which way I swam, as long as I was swimming.

'There's a picture of you somewhere, isn't there, in a pink tutu?' She nods towards the front room where the slides are kept, but doesn't move.

'That's not of me, it's of Liam. Remember, Ann and Jacinta dressed him for Halloween.' We laugh.

'God help him.'

Words float around in the air above our heads in sharp and soft focus, upper and lower casing. They are warm words, that banish disappointments and half-remembered grudges of a childhood punishment. She says again that she trusts me.

'There's something I think you should know.'

She is very still, cautious with her language. 'Something I should have told you a long time ago.' She leans forward, I can see her clearly. Her face is tense. I am suddenly afraid of her revelation. I want to be her mother, I want to protect her from the exposure, the potential embarrassment.

'Don't tell me, Mammy, if it's only the vodka that's making you.' I don't want it that way. I don't want her to think that I drew it from her in a weak moment. 'I don't want you to be sorry tomorrow.'

She sits back against the cushions, leans sideways to put her empty glass on the floor.

'All right, OK. But promise you won't think bad of me, if you ever discover a terrible thing about your mother.'

'I could never think bad of you, sure amn't I too much like you?'

There's a key in the door then. Dad makes coffee. I wash my face and straighten myself up for evening mass. Outside the church I sit on a low wall and watch the parishioners flow in. I pinch the back of my hand till I can really feel it. I try to make sense of the new things in my head, grasp what she has not told me.

In the two years that followed there were other times when I could have spoken to her, questioned her about what she'd said that day. But it seemed to me that the longer I left it, the harder it became. The whole afternoon was more like a dream to me then, the kind of dream in which the facts are jumbled but always when you wake, the feeling is the same. It's the empty feeling of an opportunity lost, when a moment of revelation slips by through ignorance of its singular importance.

When they eased her coffin into a Sutton grave and her secret leaked softly from the lips of mourners, I longed for that Sunday on the couch. I scripted again all the words in my head that had filled the room that afternoon. I rewrote the scene without caution, without the fear of judgment that had marked the space between her and me. And I mourned for the daughter I could have been if I had known the whole story.

MICHAEL CARRAGHER

Weir Way

I remember that morning because of what happened on the Weir Way, and because it was the time I got the garage. I don't remember feeling cold as I waited to be summoned to the kitchen, though I do know that my teeth were chattering because I listened to the sound, getting a strange sort of satisfaction from trying to regulate the noise; but my shivering may have been as much excitement as cold. It was dark in the bedroom, but the only thing I was scared of was that Santa might come back and take my toys away if he found that I was out of bed.

I must have been standing behind the bedroom door for a long time before I heard movement in the kitchen and timidly rattled the knob. The door opened and my father stood there, his topcoat on over his nightshirt, the candle on its saucer held high in one hand. His smile fell away when he saw the state of me.

'*Gasún, gasún*, what possessed you? Have you no sense at all?'

One of my sisters rolled over in the bed and groaned.

'You'll get pneumonia,' Daddy whispered. 'How long are you standing there?'

'Did Santa come?' was my concern, as I struggled to see round him. In the light of the candle on its saucer and the red glow of the Sacred Heart lamp on the wall, I could see only shadowy corners.

'He did to be sure, but never mind that now. You're foundered.'

He wrapped me in the folds of his topcoat – no dressing gowns in our house – and cuddled me to him. I was as cold as a wee frog, he said, my feet like two lumps of ice, and he twisted them to tuck them into the coat's pockets. The rough tweed cuffs chafed my ankles, and the coarse binder-twine uncoiling from the pockets' depths tickled my toes. I could smell the faint whiff of the farmyard off him and his own distinctive smell: that of a man who smokes and who washes himself down from the face and up from the feet as far as the flannel can reach, the same way I was to wash him in the bed years later. I never saw him in the tin bath before the hearth.

Now that hearth was cold. He wound the bellows-handle gently and a light ash rose. The pink heart of the heat deepened to cherry. Still hugging me close, he threw a handful of tinder from the tea-chest beside the hearth onto the glow. The fan-bellows again, then more fuel. Soon there was good heat, and he sat down on the upended butter-box he used as a stool and turned me to the flames. He massaged my feet and ankles in his big rough palms, and tugged each toe hard. My left foot was the colour of a candle in the firelight, and when the blood drove back through my flesh like a million tiny wedges, I cried.

'Ah my *gasún*!' Daddy whispered, kissing my curls.

'Now,' he said at last, 'let's see what Santy brought. No, Martin, you stay here.'

He rose and set me down in the armchair and draped his topcoat over me. Giddy with excitement and impatience, warm as thatch now, I looked to the corner of the kitchen where I had hung my stocking.

'Oh by the holy!' he said dramatically, and I squealed as he carried to the hearth a tube of sweets and a book with a scarlet soldier on the cover, tall black hat and moustache; a tin top with pictures painted round it: Little Red Riding Hood and a big-toothed wolf and a baby-faced man with an axe raised over his shoulder looking like he meant business, a multicoloured blur on the hearthstone when Daddy pumped the handle. The top swayed slowly on the foot-worn flag, and sang like the wind on a wire.

'And what's this?' he said, amazed, returning to the hearth with something in his arms. A grey wooden house with a bright blue roof – a doll's house, I thought for a moment of spiking terror. 'Oh, we'll have to get a good look at this,' he said, and while I peered doubtfully at what Santa had left me, he quickly pumped the Tilly lamp, dipped the tongs in methylated spirits and lit it from the candle. The flame rose blue and writhing in his hand. He clamped the tongs to the base of the lamp and the dead white mantle above turned to pale glowing yellow as the blue flame caught the envelope of gas. He hung the lamp up on its chain.

Light fell on my toy. There was a flat board shelving out in front towards two tall red petrol-pumps with round white tops, marked 'BP' and 'Mex', and in neat white letters on the roof was printed 'Martin's Garage'. Behind two sliding doors were two Dinky cars. I was thrilled to bits when I realised what Santa had given me, dumb with joy, but Daddy voiced excitement enough for both of us.

'You're in business now,' he declared. 'Selling petrol, fixing cars – oh, we'll never be poor again! But I'd better do a bit, for all that.'

He cautioned me to eat as he set out to feed the stock. I stared while the porridge cooled, at my garage on the table and my cars, the Tilly hissing cosily above. Daddy himself didn't eat: he took Holy Communion at Easter and Christmas, which meant back then that he had to fast from midnight before he could approach the altar rails. Christmas morning was the one day of the year when my mother could sleep late, for she and my sisters went to Midnight Mass, a wonderful spectacle by all accounts, with hymns, bright lights, incense, and the glamour of a late hour; but I was not allowed to go. Daddy had no notion of breaking the habits of a lifetime, and I was too old to be going like a sissy up the women's aisle and too young to go up the men's aisle by myself.

In a way I didn't mind missing Midnight Mass, for my father seemed to try to make it up to me, and the excitement of discovering what Santa had brought will always be associated with the intimacy Daddy and I shared on our Christmas morning walks. For on this day only we took the Weir Way rather than walking with the women by the road. The pigs and cattle and the mare fed, and Daddy changed into his Sunday clothes, we put on our topcoats and caps and left by the back door. The air felt cold in my body and somehow pure. The moon was as grey as a ghost and big-faced on the edge of the earth, and above the Cooley Mountains far away the blue-black sky was lightening. The few stars left seemed unusually brilliant up above the snowy slopes, and I pointed at the brightest one and said, 'That's the star that led the Wise Men to Jesus, Daddy.'

'You're the boss, Martin. I suppose you must be right.'

We went through the Pratie Garden and across the Hat Field and the Stone Field and the Long Field. A sliver of sun slipped over the rim of the mountains, bright as a sovereign that God was preparing to prise the dark lid off the world with. It was as cold as coinage too, though – no heat in it. The ground was frozen hard, only lightly floured with snow, and on the downhill slope of the Brae Field my father held my mittened small hand tightly in his big one, and cautioned me to watch my step. From the Brae Field we crossed into the Flax Field, and from there we crossed the river by the plank into the Captain's Hollow, and continued along the towpath.

The towpath was an odd name, for that river was never canalised, but maybe they ran barges along parts of it when they were building the mill and the millraces and the weir, a hundred years and more ago. A short way upriver from the plank we came to the tailrace. It was a gorgeous morning now, with the sun rising, the sky above as blue as Our Lady's mantle, as Daddy put it. Not a cloud but those of our breath. There was little enough snow on the ground down here, but Sliabh Brack up ahead was like a mountain of salt, and in the sloping fields the snow had been mounded up behind stilted tufts of cocksfoot by the northerly breeze. Against the bright blue-and-white world the branches of the trees were black, and the river was a dark brown saucy-looking streak between the hills.

My father still held my hand in his, and swapped me from side to side, breaking off his chatter from time to time to ask if I was warm. I assured him that I was, and he went on talking about the robin and its red breast, the donkey with the cross upon its back and how, with the ox, it went onto its knees every Christmas night at the hour Our Lord had been born; about how Jesus is the god of animals as well, and all the Christmas things he always told me on these walks.

'Christ!' he broke off, a short distance from the mill. 'Would you look at that fellow!' A big-haunched hare was legging up the hillside. 'If we'd thought to take the dogs – ah but sure, you couldn't take life on Christmas Day. Maybe we'll come back this way tomorrow, will we, Martin, and hunt him down?' I nodded, and he began to sing 'Adeste Fideles'.

I was very happy walking with my father on the Weir Way. I was his only child. He had married a widow much younger than he was, and he was sixty when I was born – 'the shakings of the bag', as the earthy expression had it – so he had me completely spoiled. Sometimes I'd find him staring at me, the eyes wide in his head, like a man who couldn't believe his luck. I was Daddy's Old Pal, his Wee Chirpy Cricket, his Little Fat Man – though already, at six, I was showing my mother's lanky genes. It was my father who was the little fat man, and chucklingly good-natured with it. His cheeks were ruddy and rounded, and his big brown eyes above them could look, like a child's, ready to pop out when something surprised him.

We left the towpath to scramble round the mill. The upper levels of grey limestone blocks were not yet covered by the climbing ivy, and we could see the scorch marks of the mill's destruction. After the Hitler war the market for flax fell through the floor and scutching, a local industry for centuries, was gone for ever from South Armagh. The mill's owner insured it heavily and set fire to it, and now just the stone walls were left, six or eight feet thick, with the millrace and the remains of the wheel.

As we rounded the corner and turned back down towards the headrace, our nostrils were invaded. Impaled on one of the broken spokes of the displaced waterwheel were the greenish remains of a pig. Its ribs protruded in bony bows along one side, and even in the still cold air there was a fearsome stench off it.

'Must have been brought down in the flood,' Daddy said.

A farm child, I was no stranger to death, but always fascinated by its mystery and awesome ugliness, and I stared back over my shoulder at the snarling white teeth and dark crow-plucked eye-sockets till I stumbled and was told to step up there, like a good wee man.

We could hear the water at the weir, still high after the flood, foaming over the barricade, and see its dark run as it entered the race. A strong steel mesh had been set here to save the water-wheel from being damaged by heavy debris. Now, with the mill destroyed, there was no one to clear the twigs and other flotsam that piled up and the yellow tendrils of binder-twine protruding through. Bobbing in the dark water behind the mesh was something white: the bloated body of another pig.

The path curved uphill at this point, towards McKiernan's Pass and the Lower Mountain Road and the chapel. But before we turned Daddy murmured, 'Is that Black McGarry I saw yonder?'

'I think it's Red.' I too had seen a figure move behind a tree some short distance upriver, and now it was concealed by the tidemark of dead leaves and twigs that the flood had left entangled in the lower branches and the ivy.

'God bless your eyesight, *gasún*. I never could tell them apart at this distance.'

The McGarry brothers were often taken to be twins. Tommy, the older by a year, was raven-headed; his brother, Joey, had hair the colour of liver left out in the air: almost black, but with a reddish tinge you could discern up close, or at a distance if your eyes were young and sharp, or if the sun was shining on it at an angle. They lived in a long stone house deep in the fields about a mile from us, with their rambling wild-haired mother and Tommy's wife and children. I had been cautioned not to speak to the McGarrys at school, or get near them at all, for they all had head-lice and often ringworm. They were weasel-faced and wary-eyed, unsmiling, all noticeably dirty in a time and place when no one was too clean, their noses runny on cold days, the cuffs of their threadbare cardigans and jackets shiny and stiff from wiping. Mammy had blamed them for my attack of impetigo.

'You'd wonder what he's doing here, wouldn't you?' Daddy asked as we walked on. 'He's the wrong side of the river to be going to Mass.'

'Maybe their plank was washed away,' I said.

'I wouldn't doubt it. Lazy pair, too lazy to lift it. It's a terrible thing to be a lazy man, Martin. There's Christmas come and stubble ground not ploughed. God's money's like barley in the barn, the devil's blows away like chaff . . . But God forgive me for saying bad things about my neighbours on the day that's in it.'

'Was that their pigs, Daddy?'

'Might have been. Ah, God help them. They have it awful hard, with the mother to look after, not knowing what she's going to do or when she's going to wander off. And the young missus too.'

Black McGarry's wife was a woman seldom seen, except when she appeared at the head of their long lane to berate the scholars on their way from school, over something that had been said or done to one of her children. She was a skinny creature who looked far older than she must have been, mainly because all she had to wear was what the old woman cast aside: long black skirts and moth-holed shawls. We children running past her on the far side of the road, jeering and screeching with excitement and fear, said she was a witch. 'The Wasp', our parents called her.

'We should never be off our knees, isn't that right, Martin?' Daddy went on.

'Thanking God we're on our feet, Daddy,' I said, on cue, with solemn innocence, and my father laughed.

I don't remember Mass at all – I suppose it was just more of the boring same to a child – and I skipped ahead along the Weir Way after Daddy had wished Happy Christmas to what seemed like everyone in the churchyard, and to Big Charlie McKiernan and everyone in Charlie's big family on our way down the pass. I was in a hurry to get home to Martin's Garage, and he was calling out to me to be careful and not fall. I was many yards ahead of him by the time we reached the weir. He found me waiting, staring.

'What is it, Martin?'

I didn't know. Red McGarry was standing in the river, up to his belly in the water, near where the dead pig bobbed against the mesh. He was working a long wooden pole beneath the water as a man might rake hay on the sward.

'Cross o' God!' my father murmured.

Red raised his head and looked at us through the bushes. His eyes were as wild as a colt's in a forge.

'Ah Jem, Jem, isn't this a happy Christmas!'

'What's wrong, Joey?'

'Ah, what's wrong? What's ever wrong about our place but this bitch!'

As he spoke Red hauled up on the wooden pole and held it high with one hand, then reached his other hand beneath the water.

He pulled up something white, something which I thought for a moment was another dead pig, but which I saw at once was cloth. He dropped the wooden pole and grasped the white cloth with both hands, and out of the dark water rose a woman's face, long black hair shining wet in the current, streaming through the steel mesh of the headrace with the pale strands of binder-twine.

'Oh Jesus God!' my father whispered.

Red bent down and hoisted the dead woman to his chest, and stood there in the river for some little time, looking at her. He leaned the weight on one knee and straightened out the night-dress. Then carefully, leaning to his left against the current, he stepped towards us. He waded upwater till he reached a low point of the bank.

'Can you take her, Jem?'

My father scuttled, little fat man, through the scrubby purple blackthorns and stooped down. He squatted and reached again.

'Hold on,' Red said. With one hand he reached the hem of the wet nightdress up to my father, then turned and waded back to where the wooden pole was bobbing in the water, at an angle, up against the steel mesh barricade. When he hoisted it I saw it was a salmon spear, an improvised poacher's weapon made from a worn-down shovel with two jagged V-slits hacksawed along its length. He waded back against the current, his shoulders swaying in the dark wet jacket that he wore, swinging the spear from side to side to keep his balance.

'Lift!' he shouted, as he braced the metal blade beneath the corpse.

My father leaned back, tugging on the wet cloth, and the woman's body rose out of the river with the sort of sucking splashing sound there'd been when I'd seen a foal born in the previous spring. Except this body was stiff and awkward as it hit the earth, as if it didn't fit.

Red hauled himself on to the bank, digging the spear's point in to gain purchase. My father, entranced by the sight of the dead woman, reached a hand to help too late. 'Oh my God!' he murmured. 'Oh my God!'

Then he dropped on to his knees and laid his hands on the woman's chest and leaned his weight on her.

'You're wasting your time, Jem, wasting your time,' Red said, levering one toe against the heel of the wader on his other foot. 'She's in there all night.'

Still my father pumped on the dead woman's chest. Water gushed from her mouth and nose. Her eyes were open, white and rolled back in her head. Red emptied his wader and began to work the other one off.

'I saw a child brought back from the dead this way, down at Lough Ross one time,' Daddy said.

'You're wasting your time, I tell you. Sure, she's stiff as a board. Have you the makings of a smoke about you?'

My father leaned back, fumbled in his pockets, and found a ten-pack of Aftons. He reached a cigarette to Red, who kicked the second wader off, then placed one hand inside his jacket to rub it dry, put the cigarette in his mouth, and took a light from my father's match. My father's eyes hardly left the dead woman. They were wide as a child's and his mouth was open. He reached down to pluck a long thin thread of moss, dark green and vivid, that ran like a snot from one nostril, and shook it from his hand. I was staring too: at the open white eyes and the bone-white flesh, the grey-brown nipples, sharp beneath the thin wet cloth, the distended belly and the dark bush below that shadowed through, growing up towards the navel and down between the thighs, the arms reaching stiffly for the sky.

Red puffed on his Afton, eyeing the corpse as he might a peculiar breed of bull some local man had bought against conservative advice. I noticed he was barefoot, and that the skin of his hands was purplish, and he was shivering hard, so that the cigarette wobbled in his lips. I heard my father say he'd need to watch himself or he'd catch his death of cold, and I heard Red grunt. Then I realised that his gaze was on me.

'Hardly decent to be looking at it, with a *gasún* there,' he said with a short laugh.

He took a quick puff on the cigarette, hefted the shovel, paused, laid the tool aside, and turned the corpse over with his hands. One arm had stiffened at a different angle than the other, and the corpse swayed and lurched on its knuckles and toes. He tried to steady it.

'Ah, Joey, Joey, show the dead respect!'

'Damn it, man, isn't that what I'm doing!' He puffed on the cigarette, looked at it resentfully, and threw it away – it must have got wet when he was handling the corpse.

My father turned the dead woman on her back again, took his topcoat off, and laid it on her, lining up. It covered all but her feet and her arms, which reached out and up from under it, and its bright tartan lining was loud on the land.

Red laughed again; an odd sort of laugh it seemed to me, this time.

'Well, there she is – fuckin' rotten Cooley tramp – all she ever was! Now she's done it. And how's that man going to manage without her?' He jerked his head in the vague direction of the long stone house way back in the fields.

He laughed again. Only now I realised that he was crying, and I was more dazed and horrified by that realisation than by anything else, because I'd never heard or seen a man cry in my life, least of all a tough big man like Red McGarry. I would have thought that such a thing could not be possible.

'Hell's the only place that's fit to hold her,' Red cried, his loud sobs hacking at the air, 'and her moods. It was a sad day for us all the day he took her about the place.'

My father was still staring at the dead woman there beneath

his coat, the eyes bulging in his head, as if they were trying to push the sight away from him.

'Ah, don't be saying that, Joey. It's praying for her we ought to be.' He crossed himself.

'Praying? Me poor oul' mother has her knees wore out praying for that bitch. Ah Jesus! Poor Tommy, poor Tommy! What's he going to do at all, with six wee boys and a daft oul' woman and not a thing in the house on a Christmas morning? Have you another fag there, man?'

My father reached the pale yellow pack out, and Red took it, looked in it, shook a cigarette out, broke it in two, and reached one half back to my father. My father tucked the half behind his ear. Red tossed the empty pack into the river. My father struck a match and stretched the flame.

'Would you believe me, Jem, there was weeks she went without a word out of her from Sunday to Saturday. Aye, and into Sunday again. And a face on her that would cut cold iron. That's as sure as God was born this day. A bastard's bitch. Straight out of hell.'

My father said nothing, and Red puffed in silence for a while.

'We had a few pints in Kelliher's, the two of us.' Red was calm now, his eyes on the snowy mountain. 'Got home about eleven. Went to bed.' He took a drag on the cigarette. 'He woke me about six. Told me she went out a while after he got in. To the outhouse, sure he thought, and went back to sleep.' He took another drag and threw the butt into the river at his back. 'One of the childer woke him, crying with the cold. The door was wide open; the house would skin you. She wasn't in the bed, and she wasn't in the outhouse. We checked the henhouse and the stable and the byre, and as soon as it started to get light we checked the trees. Then we set out for the river.'

'I thought I saw you, on our way to Mass.'

'You did. Here's where we started. Don't know how we missed her, but the water's deep yonder, and dark with the flood, and it was none too bright when you and the *gasún* were going past. He went downriver after that, I went up, until I knew I went too far.'

We all stood there in the blue-and-white cold, the broad saucy streak of the river at our feet and the dark branches above us splintering the sky.

'You may go home to your breakfast, Jem. Take your coat. She's warm enough without it where she is.'

My father picked his topcoat up. Red dropped his own soaking jacket on to the dead woman's face and stood barefoot looking down at her, his shoulders hunched, like a crow looking down from a wire, his jaw clacking. My father draped his topcoat over him and murmured, 'I'll get it back from you at the wake.' Red made no reply. My father reached his hand out and I took it. We set off.

Neither of us spoke until we almost reached the plank. Then: 'Hurry, Martin!'

We crossed the river, the plank springing underneath our feet above the dark run of the water. Downriver, through the bare black trees, I could see a man wading in the shallows with a pitchfork in his hands.

As we crossed the Flax Field my father took the half-cigarette from behind his ear and lit it.

'Did you ever hear of suicide, Martin, in your catechism class?' he asked quietly.

'No, Daddy.'

'Well – do you know what murder is?'

'It's when you kill someone.'

'That's right, Martin. Suicide is when you kill yourself. Now murder is an awful sin, but suicide is worse, because it's throwing the gift of life back in God's face, and it means you can never go to confession and have your sin forgiven.' We walked on, he holding my small hand tightly. 'That poor woman drowned herself.'

'I know that, Daddy.'

We crossed into the Brae Field.

'But none of us knows God's mind, Martin. And none of us knows another's mind either. God knows all, and that poor woman wasn't right in the head, so it's not a sin for her. Do you hear me?'

'Yes, Daddy.'

'Good boy. Now I want you to promise me something. Will you promise?'

'Yes, Daddy.'

'Don't ever say a word about this at school. No matter what anybody says to you. And . . . don't ever say a word against them poor motherless boys.'

'No, Daddy.'

'And don't say a word to your mother when we get in. I'll tell her.'

'No, Daddy. Daddy?'

'Yes, son?'

'Why did she kill herself?'

My father sighed very deeply. 'God knows, son. God alone knows. She had a very hard life, and maybe she figured it wasn't worth living any more. But that's always wrong.' He squeezed my hand so hard it hurt. 'You're a great boy, Martin. Did I ever tell you that? I'm grateful to God for you.'

My mother had a sharp word for us.

'What kept you? The onions are burned black. And that *gasún*'s foundered. And don't tell me you went to Mass without your topcoat? You're worse than a child.'

'Ah, it's a grand morning, Nora. And it was a long Mass. Happy Christmas, darlin'!'

I'd grown hungry, and did justice to the Christmas breakfast; it was Daddy, for once, who left his plate unscraped, and still the sight of cold steak and grease beading whitely on a plate can bring back to me the scene: my father's hand upon my mother's wrist, the low murmur of his voice, and her free hand, slowly, rising to her open mouth, and her eyes as wide as ever I have seen them.

Twenty years later I followed my father's funeral to that same church to which, on Christmas mornings, we used to take the Weir Way. The cortege took the road, of course – no one walked to Mass any more – but after the many hands were shaken by the graveside and the coffin was in the ground, I headed home alone. A meal had been laid on for the mourners at a hotel in the town, but I was able to slip away. I turned off the Mountain Road and walked down McKiernan's Pass along the slack-looped barbwire fence upon stiff tarmacadam where once a path had paralleled a hedge and muddied our shiny shoes. Along the pass were one, two, three – four houses now, in addition to McKiernan's, all tile-roofed bungalows. The people had begun to move out of the fields and towards the road when I was small.

I was resigned to the fact that my father was no longer with me. He had known that he was dying, and the knowledge was a burden he'd accepted by the end, the end a relief to both of us when it arrived. But that didn't mean I wasn't missing him. My mother had predeceased him, against all the odds, dead of cancer in middle age when he was an old man. Everyone said her death would kill him, but if it did, it took eight years, and at the end there was just him and me, together in the old house. My half-sisters were all in Dublin or in Birmingham or London, old neighbours in new houses by the road. Too absorbed in their televisions or their lives to visit more than once or twice a week, for more than a week or two after he took to his bed for the last time. We didn't miss them any more than we missed the nurse after her visits.

I worked the fields by day and sat by his bed at night until one of us dozed off. More than once he wept before my eyes. Often he spoke about my mother.

'I'd better hurry up or she'll be getting cross. Wicked woman, you know, your mother!' He winked at me merrily. 'But sure, maybe she's still too busy giving out to Larry Reilly' – my mother's first husband – 'for falling off that ladder.'

Passing McKiernan's I saw a net curtain twitch as I pressed a slack wire down and scissored a leg over it and stepped on to the grass, but I didn't look back as I walked on by the Weir Way. The fields seemed bigger than I remembered from my childhood Christmas walks, and indeed they were: only two now between the river and the road, not five. In the lower of the two, fifteen, maybe twenty acres in extent, and at the far end, there was a combine harvester clanking and droning, its steel yellow hide dulled by the dust and pollen that it worked in. The same con- tractor who had cut my own barley the week before. The crop was almost saved. A few more passes with the big machine would finish it. I walked on towards the river.

As I was coming back uphill I met Charlie McKiernan ambling down as if he were going to check on cattle or the harvesting, despite the suit he still had on from the funeral. This was Wee Charlie, a man of maybe fifty, no smaller a man than his father had been, but with a qualifier to his name whose use the grave had not worn out. He feigned surprise.

'Martin, begod!'

'I forgot about the plank,' I said, not wanting him to think either that I had gone to take the weir way out or that I'd lost my nerve.

'What's that?'

'The plank,' I said. 'There used to be a plank.'

Wee Charlie laughed. 'There was, and many's the time I crossed it. But it's gone a good while now.'

The plank across the river from our Flax Field to the Captain's

Hollow had been carried off in a flood one winter. When people walked everywhere someone always lifted river-planks before the waters rose.

'Terrible about your father, Martin,' Charlie went on, awkwardly. 'I'm sorry for your troubles.'

I could sense his annoyance: at himself for the uselessness of the words he had already muttered in the graveyard, and at me for making him be here now and making him feel the need to utter them again. When he was little more than a boy, walking in his father's shadow, Wee Charlie had famously commiserated with a widow by assuring her solemnly that her husband was 'better off away to hell out of this place anyway'. All in the wakehouse, the widow included, had responded with great mirth to his ingenuous choice of expression, and ever since he had been uncomfortable at bereavements. You'd see him slip into a wakehouse, whip his cap off as he whispered sympathy, slither headdown into the waking-room, mutter a prayer and drop a Mass card on the bed, then slip out minutes later, without as much as a sup of tea or by-your-leave; often you mightn't spot him at all.

'He had a good long life, Charlie. No regrets.'

'No, not a one. And sure he's in a better place now.'

I felt something of the same irritation Charlie must have been feeling, at the pointlessness of words at such a time. At the sanctimoniousness and – yes, hypocrisy, my own included. I was better than half of the belief that my father was simply dead; that all of him there was now was in the ground behind the church; that the loss of him was dreadful to the world, with no other world to gain from it; that life is an awful thing to have to suffer, and death no recompense; and I felt that many who would protest loudly otherwise nurtured the same fearsome suspicion. But I responded as I was supposed to.

'Smoke, Martin?' He offered an almost empty pack of Senior Service to me.

'No thanks, Charlie. They're a bit too strong for me.' I lit up one of the new tipped Carrolls that had replaced the yellow Aftons.

'They're a curse, the same bloody fags. Have us all killed.'

We were silent for a while, smoking, staring off, Charlie's mind, I feel sure, like my own, on what was waiting for us down the road. The worm in both our minds. Off at the far end of the field the combine was turning for one last slicing onslaught on the barley. Black smoke belched from its exhaust as its engine-revs rose, and as the reel began to turn the grain onto the blades something living darted on to the stubble out of the crop still standing. A hare, I thought for a moment, with surprise – for hares had been scarce for the past few years – and out of the blue I remembered the hare Daddy and I had scared up on that Christmas morning long ago. I felt the skin on the back of my neck start to tingle and my eyes begin to burn. The first bar of 'Adeste Fideles' rang in my heart. Then a cluck of rattling protest rose faintly over the chatter of the cutting-bar and the distance to our ears, and the living thing flapped frantically away. Unhappiness and dim undirected anger rose in me again.

'A pheasant,' Charlie remarked. 'Must have had a nest in there.'

The machine clanked towards us in its cloud of dust, and the last of the crop lay fallen. The diesel stumbled to a halt and the dust began to settle. A man climbed down from the driver's seat and hoisted up the reel, and a little grey Ferguson moved from the headland with a trailer, and the trailer backed up against the combine. As we watched, two men and a young lad began to drain the barley from the hopper into sacks.

'That's the way,' Charlie said. 'You'd sort of miss th' oul' mill, wouldn't you, for all the good it was?' I thought he meant the travelling mills that used to thresh the sheaves of grain in farmers' yards through the winter, but then I saw that he was looking towards the river. The scutching mill had been hauled off stone by stone as the bungalows sprang up along the slopes, to be used as back-fill.

'I mind one Christmas morning,' I began, 'the two of us came this way to Mass.'

I'm not sure why I said it. Was I challenging poor Wee Charlie to face up to it along with me? Or trying to get back at someone, anyone, for my bereavement and unhappiness and anger?

'Who? Oh, Jem, God rest him.' Charlie chuckled. 'That wasn't last year or the one before. The plank was there that time.'

'Aye.' I regretted having spoken now. I tried to find some way to finish it. 'I remember he made me a toy garage that year, out of a chair your old man sat down on and broke one time.'

Daddy had spoken of that Christmas less than a week before he'd died. 'I wasn't a bad hand with a penknife and a saw, was I?' He chuckled proudly. 'Santa needed lots of help in them days.' Then he shuddered visibly. 'Christ, I was sure you were foundered on me that morning.'

But he didn't mention what had happened on the Weir Way that self-same Christmas Day. And it struck me now, standing in discomfort with Wee Charlie, that I never had known that dead woman by her first name; that none of us ever had called her by it, or spoken much about her after she was in the ground.

Wee Charlie guffawed proudly. 'Aw-haw, no better man! And didn't care, my father, God rest him. Didn't give a damn what you said about him. Just laugh and throw it back at you. "Sure life's a joke" – that was a great saying of his – "and the man that can't have a laugh can't have much." Father Macken was making fun of him one time – malicious wee man behind that smile of his, though I shouldn't say it of a priest. "I may knock the door off the confessional," says he, "or Big Charlie'll never get that big back end of his into the box," and my father says right back, "Ah, don't be laughing at me arse, now, Father. It takes a heavy hammer to drive a big nail." Ha-ha! Brave thing to say to a priest, though, wasn't it?' He nodded and tutted lugubriously. 'Ah dear, ah dear. God be good to them all. He'll not hold that against him. I'm sure they're all in heaven. Sure we never knew anyone bad, did we, Martin?'

Anger rose red in me. Why couldn't he leave them their defiance and their poor little mortal triumphs, and not cut all that was left of them with piety and blathering fear? I took a drag on the cigarette.

'We found Red McGarry lifting Black's wife out of the water on a shovel that day, below there at the weir. Remember? The Wasp, I think they used to call her.'

Charlie turned sharply towards me, his eyes wide with surprise. He sucked air through his gapped browned teeth and turned his gaze uphill. He set off, shaking his head.

'Ah now, ah now. Don't be talking about things like that, now. Come on, I'll drive you home.'

I looked down at the weir, then turned and set off after him. My throat was hurting me. Some day Wee Charlie would be gone too, all that any of us ever have behind him, my self-centred cruelty something I could never make amends for then. We walked in silence towards the pass as I tried to find something to say. I sucked the Carrolls to the filter and flicked the butt forward off my fingernail, and Charlie took a last draw on the Senior Service and he dropped it, and we trod the tiny coals under our feet as we stepped over them. Because it was a warm dry summer, the year my father left me, and we didn't want to start a fire in the stubble.

ANNE ENRIGHT

Pale Hands I Loved, Beside the Shalimar

I had sex with this guy one Saturday night before Christmas and gave him my number and, something about him, I should have known he would be the type to call. For once, I was almost grateful that Fintan answered the phone. I could hear him through the sliding door.

'Yes, she's here. She's in the kitchen, eating dead things.' Then, 'No, I'm not a vegetarian.' Then, 'I mean dead as in dead. I mean people like you.'

I said, 'Just give me the phone, Fintan.'

After the call was finished, I threw out the rest of my dinner, came into the living room and sat down. Fintan was watching a documentary about airports, which turned out to be quite funny. When it was over, I got up to go to bed and he looked up at me and said, 'Do not go gentle,' and I said, 'Goodnight, Fintan. Goodnight, darling. Goodnight.'

I nearly went out with Fintan, before he was diagnosed. Now, we live together and people say to me, Isn't that a bit dangerous? But he is the gentlest man I know. The ashtrays were the biggest problem; the filth of them. I finally said it to him one day over the washing up, and he disappeared for a week. Then one evening he was back, sitting on the sofa with a brass box in his hand. It had the most vicious spring lid. I said, 'Where did you get that from, India?' and he looked at me. You can hear him clacking and snapping all over the house now. It's like someone smoking into a mousetrap, but it still makes me smile.

Otherwise I have no complaints. I would get him to wash his clothes more, but I think he is happier with the smell, and so am I. It reminds me of the time when I nearly loved him, back in college when it rained all the time, and no one had any heating, and the first thing you did with a man was stick your schnozz into his jumper and inhale.

These days, he is thinner and his hands tremble. He leaves his coat on around the house, and spends a lot of time looking at the air in the middle of the room – not at the ceiling or the walls, but at the air itself.

You can't trust that sort of thing. I would be the last to trust it. Personally, I don't think he is schizophrenic, but I still check his medication when he is not around. And yet – it was true what he said: when the phone rang, that night, I was eating dead things. I was sitting in the kitchen with the condensation running down the black window-pane, forking through the carbonara like it was all the men I had missed or messed up. All the men I had missed or messed up. If it was a song you could sing it. If it was a song you could play it, Sam.

I went out and took the receiver from him and said, 'Hello?' and glared at Fintan until he left the hall. 'Sorry about that.'

'Is that you?' said the guy at the other end. 'Is that you?'

So, he introduced himself – which is odd if you have slept with someone already. Then, he asked me out for 'a date'. I didn't know what to say. There was none of that when I started out. You just bumped into people. You just stayed for one more drink and then by accident until closing time, and then by a miracle, by a fumble, by something slippery and inadvertent, for the night. (But it was a serious business, this accident, I'm telling you. It was as serious as an accident with a car.) This was partly what I had been thinking in the kitchen, as the pasta slithered through the egg and the cream. 'How do I do this now? How do I crash the goddamn car?'

'So, what about Friday night?' he said.

'Sorry?'

'Or Wednesday?'

So I checked the imaginary diary in the darkness of the hall, and listened for a while to the dial tone, after he had put down the phone.

I wasn't sure that I liked him. That was all.

The dinner was hilarious. I should stop whining about my life, but I sat in a restaurant with red velvet curtains and white linen tablecloths and expensive, smirking waiters, and wondered, as I played with the fish knife, what all this was *for*. We went back to his place and I could feel the migraine coming through the sex. It should have been nice – I have no objection to sex – but with the migraine starting I felt as though he was a long way away from me, and every thrust set my brain flaring until I was very small and curled up, somehow, at the bottom of my own personal well.

Of course he was very solicitous and insisted on driving me home. Men say they want casual sex, but when you say thanks-very-much-goodnight they get quite insulted, I find. So he touched the side of my face and asked could he see me again, and when I said yes he undid the central locking system with a hiss and a clunk, and let me go.

In the kitchen I drank four cups of kick-ass black coffee, and went to bed. And waited.

Some time the next day, Fintan came in and closed the curtains where there was a little burn of light coming through. I was so happy the light was gone, I started to cry. There is something unbelievable about a migraine. You lie there and can't believe it. You lie there, rigid with unbelief, like an atheist in hell.

Fintan settled himself on a chair beside the bed and started to read to me. I didn't mind. I could hear everything and understand everything, but the words slid by. He was holding my childhood copy of *Alice in Wonderland* and I wondered were the colours that intense when I was young; Alice's hair a shouting yellow, the flamingo scalded pink in her arms.

He got to the bit about the three sisters who lived in the treacle well – Elsie, Lacie, and Tillie. And what did they live on? Treacle.

' "They couldn't have done that, you know," Alice said, "they'd have been ill." '

' "So they were," said the Dormouse. "VERY ill." '

I smiled, swamped by self-pity. And suddenly I got it – clear as clear – the smell of treacle, like a joke. The room was full of it. Sweet and burnt. It was a dilation of the air: it was a pebble dropped into the pool of my mind, so that, by the time the last ripple had faded, the pain was gone or thinking of going. The pain was possible once again.

'Oh,' I said.

'What?' said Fintan.

He looked at me in the half-dark. Downstairs, the phone began to ring. I went to get out of bed but Fintan stopped me, just by the way he sat there, in a chair by my side.

A couple of weeks later I was arguing with him, banging his dirty dishes in the kitchen. It is possible Fintan has a problem with water. It is possible all men have a problem with water. Someday they will find the gene for it, but in the meantime, I want a better life.

But of course Fintan never answers back, so the argument is always about something else – something you can't quite put your finger on. The argument is about everything.

Yes, I wanted to say, he is married. But he is separated – well and legally separated – from a wife who is always sick; a daughter who is bright but will not eat; another daughter who is his pride and joy. I liked him: he made the effort. Every time we met, there was some present: usually not to my taste, but 'tasteful' all the same; small and expensive, like some moment from a fifties film. And there was an astonishing darkness in bed. That had to be said. I felt, as he reared away from me, that he was thinking about nothing, that there were no words in his head. He rolled his eyes back into it, and the widening dark was bliss to him. It was like watching a man die. It was like having sex with an animal.

None of which I said as I banged the saucepan from Fintan's scrambled eggs on to the draining board. I didn't mention the too-bright daughters either, or the crumbling ex-wife. What I did say was that Fintan had to find somewhere for the Christmas holidays, because I didn't want to be worried about him in the house by himself.

'Christmas doesn't matter,' he said.

'Right.'

Of course not. Christmas, I went down home. What mattered was the New Year, because when midnight struck I would be in an hotel, drinking good champagne beside bad swagged curtains. I would be in bed with my new squeeze, my big old, hairy old, Mister Daddy-O.

And. And. And.

'And I don't mind your dishes, Fintan, but I really can't take scrambled egg.'

There was a silence.

'Fried?'

'Fried is fine.'

He was right. Fintan didn't care about the champagne, or even about the curtains. I suspect he wasn't even bothered by the sex. He cared about something else. A small flame that he put his hands around, but could not touch.

He is the gentlest man I know.

But it was a gentle feeling I had, too. I wanted to say that, somehow – that this man had too much money and no taste, but he wanted me very hard. I wanted to say how helpless this made him; how violent and grateful I felt him to be. I wanted to say that he had flat, self-important eyes but the back of his neck smelt like a baby's hair.

That evening, as I opened the front gate, I heard the sound of the piano starting up in the house behind me. It was dusk. Across the road, the alcoholic teacher had put up his Christmas lights; a different shape in each of the windows. There was a square and a circle downstairs, upstairs a triangle and what we used to call a rhomboid, all in running, flashing, gold and white. Over by the post box, an object flew out from among a cluster of boys and landed in the roadway. It was a skateboard. I stood there with my hand on the cold, low handle of the gate and listened to the first bars of the *Pathetique*.

You only play when I'm not looking, I thought. Every time I look, you stop.

I stood at the bus stop, but as soon as the bus appeared I pulled my coat around me and walked back to the house. Because, if he was playing again, then the shake was gone from his hands. And if the shake was gone then he was off his pills and all hell was about to be let loose – airport police, Fintan running naked through Dublin or, if he was lucky, Paris; Fintan balanced on the parapets of buildings or bridges, with his pockets full of rocks.

I had never seen him in full flower. I was away when it started, the summer after our finals – in which, of course, he had done indecently well. His notes, they discovered later, were written all in different colours, and some were in code. There was a dried-out pool of blue ink draining out of the bath, staining the enamel. It was still there when I got back to the house – hugely sad. The blue of his thoughts, the blood of his mind, I thought, as I tried to scrub it away and failed, or sat in the bathwater and looked at it.

So when he came out of hospital six months later his room was still there, as it should be. No one was going to let Fintan down.

Our other housemate (and my ex), Pat, was setting something up in Germany and was always there and gone again. I had a job. Over the years, the area started to come up. And then it was just Fintan and me.

Now it was just me, crying on the way back from the bus-stop, pulled by the sound of his playing along a terrace of pebble-dash, painted blue and grey and dark green. The woman we called Bubbles was listening at her front door in a peach-coloured housecoat-negligée. She saw me blowing my nose and I gave her a laugh and waved her away. I didn't know what I was crying for. For the music. For the guy I used to know at college, maybe, with his boy's body and his jumper of royal blue. And the fact, I think, that his were the first hands I ever loved, the whiteness of them.

The playing stopped as I put my key in the door. When I got into the living room he was sitting on the sofa, as though he had never left it. I pulled him into an awkward, easy embrace and we sat like that, Fintan twisted into me, his face pressed against my chest until my T-shirt was wet from the looseness of his mouth. We sat for a long time. We made that picture of ourselves. That pietà. When I closed my eyes, I could see us sitting there – though I could not, for some reason, feel him in my arms.

In the kitchen, drinking tea, the phone started to ring. I went out to answer it, and then I came back and sat down.

'I used to be clever, Fintan,' I said. 'But it is no use to me any more.'

'I know,' he said.

I should have given him his pills then. I should have forced one into his hand, into his mouth, or down his throat – but we were always too delicate with each other, even for words, so we just said goodnight and went to bed.

On Christmas Day, my mother announced that plum pudding was too much trouble any more, and produced one of those shop-bought ice-cream desserts. My brother had brought a few good bottles of wine, and I supplied the paper hats. After the pudding declaration, we had a huge fight about brandy butter and I burst into tears. My mother just looked at me.

On New Year's Eve, I rang the house, but there was no answer. And when I got home on the third of January, Fintan was gone.

On the fourteenth of February I got my Valentine's card by registered post and twelve fat, dark roses delivered to my desk at work. I also got a phone call from Fintan's occasional brother in Castleknock to say that they had found him, finally, that they knew where he was.

I took the afternoon off and bought a Discman and some CDs, then took a taxi out to Grangegorman. I had never been there before: it was a joke of an asylum, looming and Victorian, people muttering and whining in the bare wards, and a smell everywhere of bleach and sperm that was like your own madness, not theirs. When I found him, Fintan was lying so still in the bed that you could see every bump and crevice, from the knuckles of his fingers to the high, tender line of his penis, under the thin white counterpane. He opened his eyes and closed them again. Then he opened them and looked at me for a while and turned his head away. Drugged up to the eyeballs.

I clipped the headphones into his ears and put some music into the Discman. He twitched, and I turned the volume down. Then he turned to look at me, as the music played. He took my hand and placed it against his face, over his mouth and nose, and he kissed my palm. He looked at me with great love. I don't know what his eyes said as they gazed at me, over my lightly gagging hand. I don't know what they saw. They saw something lovely, something truly lovely. But I am not sure that they saw me.

The wedding was in November, by which time Fintan was back in the world again, slightly depleted. Every time this happened, I thought, he would become more vague; harder to see. I felt many things – guilt mostly – but the Health Worker wanted to put him in a halfway hostel, and besides, I was leaving. Whatever way you looked at it, the house was finished for us now. There would be no more snapping ashtrays and trips to the launderette, there would be no more evenings on the bust-up sofa, or chats with Bubbles on the Captain's Road.

But I never once thought of saying goodbye to him. I was only getting married. I even brought him along on the hen night – as a sort of mascot, I suppose.

The evening started off slow. My grown-up girlfriends were talking contact numbers and exchanging business cards – I had to start the Tequila slammers myself. Two hours later we were off – the Final Bash, the last night ever. I have some recollection of a couple of horse-drawn cabs. I also remember climbing in over the back wall of my new, that is to say, my future husband's house. It did not occur to us – to any of us – to use my key, or even knock at the front door. There was a light on in the kitchen: I remember that. We stripped a red-brick wall of ivy and wore it in our hair. I lost my knickers to some ritual in the flower beds. My oldest friend Cara took pictures, so this is how I know all this – two of the girls trying to get my shirt off, Breda ripping up the dahlias (saying, apparently, 'Boring flowers. Boring flowers') and someone, it looks like Jackie, snogging Fintan up against a tree. In the photo, he is all throat. His head is bent back for the kiss, so the flash catches his adam's apple and the blue-white underskin of his neck.

I kissed him myself once. It was in my second year at college, before he went mad, or whatever. We sat on the windowsill at a party and pulled the curtains around us and talked for a while, with our heads tipped against the cold windowpane. I remember the silence outside, the curtains resting against us, and beyond them the fug and blather of the room. At some stage, I kissed him. And that was all. The skin of his mouth was terribly thin. Even then, Fintan dealt in moments. As though he moved through liquid while the rest of us made do with air.

So, I am married, whatever that means. I think it means that now I know.

Now I am living in that house with its boring flowers and ivy-covered walls, I know that I didn't 'nearly' love Fintan – I loved him, full stop. And there is nothing I can do about it – about the fact that I loved him for years and did not know it. Nothing at all.

I sleep easy enough beside my husband, my greedy old man. Because he was right in a way – Fintan is always right, in a way. So many of the men that you meet are dead. Some of them are dead in a nice sort of way, some of them are just dead. It makes them easy to seduce. It makes them dangerous to seduce. They give you their white blindness.

So it is easy, under the sheets, to lie beside him and think about nothing much. My hairy old baby. Who would do anything for me. He spends money on me, it seems to give him pleasure – more pleasure than what he is buying at the day's end, because dead men don't know the difference between things that are alive (me, for example, or even my cunt) and things that are dead, namely his money, which is just so many dried-out turds and not worth living in the house of the dead for. And so I keep talking and he keeps dying, and giving me things that have already decayed (a 'lovely' silk scarf, a car that I might want to drive someplace, two books that are quite like real books I might want to read). There is the conspiracy of the dead all around us and the head waiters still smirk, as head waiters do, while the food fucks on the table-top in an encouraging sort of way.

I am sick now. This life does not suit me. His old wife has cyst problems, something horrible with her back, some disintegration. I hear her silence on the other end of the phone. I see the chequebook with her name in it, printed under his. I am thinner now. My clothes are more expensive. Weekends he sees his daughters – always a little bit better at their maths, their smiles always sweeter, their ribbons that little bit straighter, their cheekbones beginning to break through the skin of their faces now, too early, beautiful and aghast.

I meet Fintan in the afternoons and we have sex sweet as rainwater. I need the sun more than anything and we undress in the light. I open the curtains and look towards the sea. He is madder now than he ever was. I think he is quite mad. He is barely there. Behind my back I hear the sound of threads snapping. I turn to him, curled up on the sheet in the afternoon light, the line of bones knuckling down his back, the sinews curving up behind his knees and, trembling on the pillow, casually strewn, the most beautiful pair of hands in the world.

I say to him, 'I wish I had a name like yours. When I'm talking to you, you're always "Fintan". It's always "Fintan this", "Fintan that". But you never say my name. You know? Sometimes I think you don't actually know it – that no-one does. Except maybe him. I listen out for it, you know?'

JANE S. FLYNN

Halcyon Day

There's a rosy cloud sitting on Hag's Head and Inishmore is floating on the horizon, all blue and ochre.

'By the hokey, I can't believe it. A good day!' I say, stretching over my desk to get a right grip on the drapes. 'Inishmore looks like a whale basking in the sun.'

'A pet day,' he murmurs.

'Maybe it's a halcyon. That's an unseasonable calm around the Christmas,' I say, paraphrasing an article from yesterday's *Times*. I use 'the Christmas' for 'the Solstice' to take the harm out of the big words and short-circuit any connection with New Agers ('Silly cunts,' he calls them, irrespective of gender), and launch into a synopsis of the Greek myth: 'Alcyone loved her husband so much that after he died, the gods pitied her and turned them both into kingfishers that nested in the winter calm between storms' – but he's already back to sleep ('I love the bed,' he brags shamelessly), so I face into the cold kitchen.

While the porridge cooks I hang out wash that's been folded in the wicker basket waiting out gales. This December day hardly a puff shimmies around the battered whitewashed gable. Gravity unlumps the fringe on my Early American tablecloth and the shadows from the Supercale sheets (forty years old this coming May, the same age I was when I came here) stretch all the way into the middle of the next field, perfectly still. The sun is climbing and the sky is pink and there are two stunted sprigs of lavender blooming in the herb garden (they weren't there when I searched for sage and fennel for soup) which I pick, to press. Two witnesses to the lull. To the halcyon. A halcyon must be the opposite of a cyclone, I muse. Has it anything to do with anticyclones? And depressions? I must look it up. I'll end up as bad as my father, looking everything up.

Halcyon, the Dove goddess and the leader of the Pleiades constellation, says the Women's Mythology book, was associated with the two solstices as Life-in-Death and Death-in-Life. This is particularly meaningful to me as my birthday is the very day of the solstice, the shortest day of the year, December 21. 'My name is Irene and I will be sixty,' I keep saying, like somebody in AA, and still I don't believe it. I can't really be that old.

'Porridge is ready,' I shout. He comes to the table so quickly I know he has been awake, just waiting for the call. After taking his heart tablets (for the cardiac infarct he euphemistically terms 'a warning') he dumps two heaping tablespoons of sugar over the oatmeal, and ignoring the litre of low-fat milk next to his mug, floods the bowl to the rim with full cream milk from the coffee pitcher. He eschews moderation. 'When I'm out, I'm out,' he says.

My chair faces the biggest window in the house. When the sun is out I can sometimes see the Kerry mountains, but today my eyes lock on the scatter of feathers stuck to the briars outside our thorny wire, so white and clean and fluffy they look like wisps of angel hair. Three weeks ago the Silkey bantam hen was killed while we were in town. He blamed a dog. 'A dog on the ramble,' was the phrase. She had a little top-knot and turquoise dots on either side of her head like my Navajo earrings.

'I'm counting the days till the hens start laying,' he says. 'That brown lady will cover a great clutch.'

The sun shows up every pothole in the drowned land. Mirror shards, they look like, and the boggy swamp beside the cattle trough is a dazzling silver serpentine.

'You know what we'll do today? We'll put up the Christmas trimmings,' he says.

He makes a big deal out of Christmas. If it was just myself I wouldn't bother at all. I am no longer religious in the orthodox sense of the word and the secular celebration known as 'the holiday season' only reminds me of Walt Disney and Johnny Mathis roasting Rudolf's chestnuts red white and blue at the mall.

While he sorts through junk boxes for the fairy lights, I open windows. You have to blow the must out of these old stone houses every chance you get. Sunlight streams in, illuminating swarms of dust and turf ash and smutty cobwebs.

'Oh. That ceiling,' I say. It sags and is peppered with mildew.

'Forget it. Don't look.' He anticipates my next line about wiping it down. We are together so much one knows what the other is thinking. I'm glad he dismisses the idea because the very thought of it makes my neck hurt. Last summer, one mesmeric starry night, I watched comets for so long I finished up in a cervical collar. 'Jewish necklaces,' we used to call them.

He plugs in the string of lights. Nothing happens.

'Check for loose bulbs. These are dear ones,' he says. They were salvaged from the bin of an old lady (RIP) renowned locally for her parsimony.

'I'll never know how she spent so much on them. She was as tight as a fish's hole. And that's watertight.'

We twist each fragile lantern one by one, he from the plug end, me from the top. He is determined to get them going, winking green and red and yellow until Small Christmas. Epiphany, that is.

'Hi! Is that thing still plugged in?' He disconnects. 'Show. One's missing.'

I spot a minuscule glass vial on the floor and screw it in.

'Perfect,' he declares.

'Why don't we put them in the porch?' I suggest. The porch window is larger and only a few will show from here, unless he cross-hatches them back and forth English Tudor style, like he did the evergreens last year. He says his mother always dressed the old shutters and sills with red Christmas paper, then tacked string over them, like a lattice, for holly and ivy. Crêpe paper, I bet it was.

'Get me the box to stand on.'

'The box,' another lucky find, is encrusted with the petrified remains of barrnock shells and is kept outside the back door, weighted down with a big sea stone. 'Yassa,' I say, shuffling off like Steppin Fetchit. I've told him about Steppin Fetchit.

The sun is strobing in the southwest and three small boats are puttering around the cliffs below. Lobster fishermen from Liscannor, they would be, out for a Christmas bonus. The tide must be fully in.

When I return, the tool box is open and he is hammering clips mooched from the ESB lads into the window casing. He's always on the lookout for stuff for this box, which is 'his' even though I purchased it for 'the house.' All incoming hardware is his by default, even cup hooks, and he knows every time I've touched anything.

'Do you think you should allow for some slack?'

'Get me a screwdriver,' he replies, and immediately twiddles that brain-piercing whistle he knows I hate (that and the three cast-iron clangs of the fire tongs after every turf adjustment, 'to clean the ashes,' he says) and without pausing for breath continues, 'It's true, that about Mikey Barry Mac. They don't give him a chance, the poor hoor. And what harm, but he's leaving a fine wife behind him.'

Mikey Mac owns the bog where we get our turf. His face is purple-black, like he was just strangled. I stare out the window into the swelled, rushy fields between our house and the sea. The ocean, pure ultramarine, is so flat you can't tell what way the tide is now, and there is a lapis lazuli plane above the horizon the clouds are sitting on, all bunched up, then billowing, then teased into oblivion.

'What?' he prompts.

'Nothing. I didn't say anything.'

He's always filling in pauses. 'Anything's better than cursing,' and 'Won't we be laying head to foot to one another soon enough and not able to say a word?' he always says. I don't tell him everything I'm thinking. Often I'm not thinking, only stopped in mid-consciousness somewhere neither here nor there.

Next we do the electric candles. There are three of them, set into split pine blocks decorated with robins and sparkles. He bought one for every window on the saluting side of the house.

'Where does this one go?' I ask. It has no plug top.

'Our bedroom.'

'Right. I'll move my stuff.' I wince like I do when he wants the heavy extension cord the printer's on. My stuff is on my side of the bed. The computer and printer are on my desk facing out on to the driveway he calls 'the street'. The sill is full of pens and pencils and literary effects which I proceed to clear, to make room for the candle. Before I am finished, he is pulling the rug up under my feet, getting at leads.

'What are you doing? Don't disconnect my computer. Leave those things the way I have them.' The computer is American and uses a transformer. I am mortally afraid something will go wrong and they won't be able to fix it here.

He has a screwdriver in one hand. 'I'll use the lamp,' he says. There is only one receptacle plate in the room. It has two sockets. The transformer has an outlet to itself. The printer, radio, and bedside lamp share a square adapter. Everything is labelled to avoid disaster. He is going to hot-wire the Christmas candle on to the lamp, I realise.

'Will you just please tell me what are you going to do with those two bare wires?' I ask, enunciating every phoneme.

'I'm going to fix the Christmas candle. Pull the hangings. I can't see a stab for that fucking sun.'

'I don't want any Rube Goldberg jobs around that computer,' I declare, and as that expression of my father's leaves my lips (it is surely inspired) I relax, and I prepare to tell him about the cartoon character after he asks 'What's that?' but he doesn't. He says nothing at all because he is thinking 'I won't please her by asking.'

'Why can't you just put a proper plug on that plugs in and out? That candle will only be on a few hours at night when I'm not using the computer.'

'I don't have one and besides, you don't need it,' he says.

I know he is jealous of the computer. He is always interrupting me, barging in with reports of who's on Clare FM when I'm writing.

'Please. Leave it. I'll get a plug. I'll buy one.' I stress 'buy'.

'Right. So. You know, this isn't a Paddy-me-arse job. That candle . . .' he shakes it for emphasis, '. . . that candle has a switch that can be turned on and off.'

He leaves the room then, just walks out with the bed and night table and desk arsewise and electric cords strewn around and starts putting a fire down. I clean up the mess, then go outside and stay there watching the sun set, watching the white ribbon scrolling over the reef in front of Hag's Head, watching a last splink of fluorescent red-orange vibrate and melt down into the sea, watching for the green flash called the living light. 'Whoever sees it will never be deceived in matters of the heart,' says the folklore book.

When I step inside, the room is full of smoke, belching blow downs. He always lays the sods cocking out towards the front, away from the draught. I think he does it on purpose to hear me say 'It's smoking, again'. The tools are all on his side – tongs, poker, brush, fire lighters and turf basket.

As I boil the kettle for the hot-water bottle, the moon is a copper crescent in the southwest. It is lit from underneath, I decide, because the sun has sunk. Turned on its back, it looks like a cradle rocking. He is shoving the fire back, pulling our chairs away from the hearth. 'The moon is like the one in Winken, Blynken, and Nod,' I call in to him.

Before I turn off the kitchen light the moon is gone and the sky is marvellous. It is bitter cold. The picture window is dripping with condensation and I dry a circle with the curtain in time to see a meteor shoot into the west, then another. There are so many stars I can't pick out constellations. My neck crackles. I have a last look out the back door. The Big Dipper is there. Usually it's over Liscannor scooping up the North Star at the Cliffs of Moher. I would go outside to hunt for the Pleiades (a subtle lot, I look at them indirectly) but it is too cold.

'Bring me a glass of spring water,' he calls from the bedroom, chanting like High Mass. I never have a foot on the floor that he doesn't think of something he wants.

I see Inishmore lighthouse spark, and wait for the next throb, counting out the thirteen seconds between pulses. One summer night ten years ago I saw the beacon swirl completely around. It felt like less time than thirteen seconds, though.

When I join him under the two down quilts, he is warm and redolent in his striped pyjamas. 'My hospital pyjamas,' he calls them.

'Your little cushcamers are like two blocks of ice,' he says. (That's Irish for little feet – an expression of his mother's.) 'These bloody clothes would perish you.' Flannel ones like babycrib sheets, he wants. Mine are heavy white cotton percale, line-dried and ironed smooth as an altar cloth.

'Here, take the bottle over to your side,' he says, kicking it towards me.

'No, it's OK.' I'm afraid of getting chilblains again. I hadn't a clue what they were before I moved here. Or 'Ah-Bee-Cees'. How did I ever stick it out that first winter? I must have been mad. He smells like turf. He used to smell like cigarettes. The night he got the attack I buried my face in his sweater when I got back from the hospital. Red lambswool it was, reeking of him, tobacco and smoke and sweat and porter. He still smokes when I'm not around. 'I take the odd pull of a fag,' he told the doctor lately, in front of me. Clever boots. Killing two birds. He isn't fooling him, either.

'Is it making frost?' he asks. 'I love hard frosty weather.'

'I don't know. I was looking at stars.' I press my thumbs and forefingers together Yoga style and resolve to check my Starfinder programme for Halcyon.

'If it's dry tomorrow we'll take a spin to the blessed well for holly and ivy.'

St Joseph's well, festooned with scapulars and old rosary beads and cloth tatters tied to the bushes. 'OK,' I say, and, 'Oh. We forgot to turn the fairy lights and candles on.'

'I didn't forget, and you should have left this one on the light plug.'

The computer hums, fleshing out the silence. The glass bead is amber for hibernation mode, and under the desk the red plastic button on the Monster Surge control glows spooky red. Vigil lamps, I realise, and bite my lips holding in ·a laugh, then turn into his back – we are a perfect fit – and curve around him filling his hollows and slide my hand under his arm, across his wheezy chest, over his heart. We have been sleeping together for twenty years. I can't imagine being alone again. Being lonely. 'Lonesome,' he says. 'Wouldn't it make you pure lonesome . . .'

BIOGRAPHICAL NOTES

KEVIN BARRY was born in Limerick in 1969. He is now based in Cork where he is a freelance journalist. 'Miami Vice' is his first story to be published.

MICHAEL CARRAGHER was born in Newry, Co. Down, in 1953. He was educated locally and at Trinity College, Dublin, and he has a degree in fiction writing from the University of Arkansas and from Louisiana State University. His first story appeared in the *Irish Press* 'New Irish Writing' in 1984, and since then he has had stories published in the US and the UK. His debut collection, *A World Full of Places*, was published by Blackstaff Press.

ANNE ENRIGHT was born in Dublin in 1962 and educated at Trinity College, Dublin and the University of East Anglia. Her highly praised debut story collection, *The Portable Virgin*, won the Rooney Award, and she has since published two novels, *The Wig My Father Wore* and *What Are You Like?* She works as a television producer at RTE.

JOHN FLEMING was born in Dublin in 1964. He works there as a web site editor and copywriter, having worked in Paris, New York and London. His radio plays and short stories have been broadcast on RTE, BBC 3 and BBC World Service.

JANE S. FLYNN was born in Atlantic City, USA, of Irish-American parents, and is a graduate of Temple University, Philadelphia. She moved to Ireland in 1978 and married a traditional singer from Co. Clare. She won the *Image*/Oil of Ulay short story competition and in 1996 had a story in the first *Phoenix Irish Short Stories*.

FIONA GARTLAND was born in Dublin in 1967. She has had stories in magazines and a play on community radio.

WILLIAM HODDER was born in the North Parish, Cork City, in 1951 and is a graduate of University College, Cork. He writes poetry and fiction in both Irish and English, and his first verse collection in Irish was published by Coiscéim in 1996. A teacher of Irish, Latin and Religion, he had a story in the 1999 *Phoenix Irish Short Stories*.

CORMAC JAMES was born in Cork in 1971. He has had stories published in the UK and US and has also translated a collection of Polish poetry. His first novel, *Track & Field*, was published last year by New Island Books. He now lives and works in Dublin.

MARY LELAND was born in Cork where she lives and works as a freelance journalist, mainly for the *Irish Times*. Her first stories appeared in the *Irish Press* 'New Irish Writing' and she published her first novel, *The Killeen*, in 1985. This was followed by a short story collection, *The Little Galloway Girls*, and a second novel, *Approaching Priests*.

SEÁN MacMATHÚNA was born in Co. Kerry and now lives in Dublin where he has taught at both second and third levels. He has published two short story collections in Irish, and *The Atheist*, his first collection in English, was published in 1987 by Wolfhound Press.

MOLLY McCLOSKEY was born in Philadelphia in 1964. She studied English Literature at St Joseph's University, Philadelphia, and moved to Co. Sligo in 1989. She won the George A. Birmingham Short Story Award both in 1991 and 1994, and the RTE/Francis MacManus Award in 1995. She had a story in the 1996 *Phoenix Irish Short Stories* and in 1997 Phoenix published her first collection, *Solomon's Seal*.

BRIAN McKILLOP was born in Carnlough, Co. Antrim, in 1976 and educated locally at St MacNissis College. He has travelled in the US and Europe, and worked as an apprentice joiner, welder, taxi receptionist, and antique salesman. 'Pane Barrier' is his first story to be published.

GILLMAN NOONAN was born in Kanturk, Co. Cork, and is a graduate of University College, Cork. He has worked widely in Europe, particularly in Germany and Switzerland. His first stories appeared in the *Irish Press* 'New Irish Writing', and Poolbeg Press published his two collections, *A Sexual Relationship* and *Friends and Occasional Lovers*. He won the Writers' Week Short Story Award in 1996.

WILLIAM TREVOR was born in Mitchelstown, Co. Cork, and is widely regarded as the greatest living writer of short stories. He has published ten collections, the latest being *The Hill Bachelors*, published in 2000. He is also the author of twelve novels, two novellas, a play, a book of non-fiction and a children's book. He has won many prestigious literary awards and in 1997 was awarded an honorary CBE in recognition of his valuable services to literature, and in 1999 received the David Cohen British Literature Prize in recognition of his lifetime's literary achievements.

AUGUSTUS YOUNG was born in Cork in 1943. His poems and short stories have been published in Ireland and Britain, and extracts from a novel appeared in the *London Magazine*. Two novellas with a memoir, *The Making of a Moderately Useful Life*, are due for future publication.

WILLIAM WALL was born in Whitegate, Co. Cork, in 1955. A graduate of University College, Cork, he is a teacher. His first stories appeared in the *Irish Press* 'New Irish Writing' and his first poetry collection came out in 1997. Sceptre published his two novels, *Alice Falling* (2000), and *Minding Children* (2001).

Previously unpublished short stories are invited for consideration for future volumes of *Phoenix Irish Short Stories*. Unsuitable MSS will not be returned unless a stamped, addressed envelope is enclosed. Writers outside the Republic of Ireland are reminded that, in the absence of Irish stamps, return postage must be covered by International Reply Coupons: two coupons for packages up to 100g, three for packages 101g to 250g. All communications regarding MSS which require a reply must be accompanied by a self-addressed envelope and return postage. MSS and letters should be addressed to David Marcus, PO Box 4937, Rathmines, Dublin 6.